Julie Valentine
1982

The View from the Window

By the same author

NOBODY'S GARDEN
A CAT CALLED CAMOUFLAGE

Cordelia Jones

THE VIEW FROM THE WINDOW

ANDRE DEUTSCH

First published 1978 by
André Deutsch Limited
105 Great Russell Street London WC1

Copyright © 1978 by Cordelia Jones
All rights reserved

Printed in Great Britain by
Bristol Typesetting Company Ltd
Bristol

British Library Cataloguing in Publication Data

Jones, Cordelia
The view from the window.
I. Rheumatoid arthritis in children –
Juvenile literature
I. Title
362.7'8'196720924   RJ482.A77

ISBN 0–233–97004–5

The Hospital in this story is not based on any real hospital and all the characters are totally fictitious.

Chapter I

THE only redeeming feature of Granstead hospital was the view from the windows. Although that part of Essex, close to the Suffolk border, was getting more and more built up at this time, towards the end of the 1960s, the hospital still looked out over unspoilt country with scarcely a house in sight. There was a good view to the west, especially in the evening when the light was waning and the endless country, gently rolling and wooded here and there, led into the sunset like the end of a sentimental film; like so many things which seem trite in a film or a picture, there was nothing sentimental about the dusk skies over this stretch of rolling country. Nobody else bothered to look at them, nor could they understand why Irene would sit for hours in the darkening dayroom, doing nothing, when everyone else had come back into the ward to watch television.

But that was the last time she had been in hospital. This time she had been given one of the high beds. This meant that she had to go to bed soon after four, the only time when there were two nurses available to lift her on to the bed. Irene had rheumatoid arthritis; almost all her joints were affected and there was so little movement in her hips that she was quite incapable of scrambling up on to the high bed by herself. Fortunately her bed was alongside the window. Although the hospital was a gaunt early nineteenth-century building, some unexpectedly imaginative architect had put the windows low enough to be looked out of, even from bed. Her view was to the north, out over the laundry buildings, boiler house, coal bunkers, and bicycle sheds, and a bonfire where they burnt what seemed to be an inexhaustible supply of defunct hospital furniture, and then across a field of beet to where a little wood lay folded in the rural landscape. There was a lane winding into it and another skirting it, crossing her view from right to left. It was a little wood of oaks with close frilly foliage, a few horse chestnuts, one or two beech trees and some tall larches.

'It's like a wood out of a picture,' said Irene, 'perhaps because it's small enough to go in all in one piece.'

'Yes,' said her uncle William, 'it might almost be Gainsborough's *Cornard Wood*. Perhaps that's just because the late summer has given it the golden tone of an eighteenth-century landscape. It's the oaks too, with the odd gesticulatory dead branch — just what the East Anglian landscapists loved. And the sandy lane winding into the wood, borrowed from Dutch painting. Even the little figures — they are probably painted in by another hand, some painter who specialised in staffage.'

Irene smiled. It was her uncle who had taught her to see things as pictures. When she pointed out the sunlight falling into the kitchen as seen down the passage from the front hall, he would murmur 'Pieter de Hooch.' Always he had some picture, or else a poem, to match what she had seen. 'It's like a picture to me because I shall never go there,' she said. 'I can't get through the picture frame. There are some painters, aren't there, who try to make you feel as if you were inside the painting? This isn't that sort of landscape.'

Her uncle leant against the window sill. 'Perhaps that's what makes it look like an eighteenth-century landscape. It's self-contained. There's no foreground you could step into. It's like a vignette.'

'I love the little figures,' said Irene, 'even if they are painted by another hand. Sometimes a riding school passes, lots of girls on horseback. I don't think I care for landscape without figures. But they are all thumb-sized people out there — not people I shall ever meet. They have no connection with our closed world in hospital.'

'Up and down the people go,'

8

he began to quote uncertainly. 'I never cared much for Tennyson so I can't remember how it goes.

"I am half sick of shadows," said
The Lady of Shalott.

Did you read it at school? She sits weaving a tapestry or "magic web" and only sees the real world reflected in a mirror. It's like the way you described the people on that lane out there – she sees the people go by "down to towered Camelot" and she weaves "the mirror's magic sights" into her web.'

'But she wanted to see the real thing, didn't she?' said Irene with a sigh.

He noticed the sigh. 'I daresay if you got to the wood it wouldn't be worth it. There's probably a motor road just hidden from sight. And those little figures would be just like anyone in hospital if you met them. The magic web is always far more beautiful than the reality.' He was always urging her to write, yet Irene had no impulse to put words on to paper. She knew he would speak of it now. 'You must weave a little web,' he said. 'You could even make something beautiful out of this dreary place.' He cast his eye mockingly round the hospital interior, the pale green paint to shoulder height and cream above.

He wants me to snap out of this mood, thought Irene. But somehow she couldn't. 'You're wrong about me,' she said. 'I'm not a maker. I only want to live – just an ordinary life in an ordinary world. There was some curse, wasn't there?' she added. It began to come back to her. They had read it in her last year at school, when she was already ill but while drugs kept her mobile, before she had had to give up the struggle to live a normal life. Everything that had happened that year had a curious surreal clarity as if she had watched herself live it from a distance.

Yes, she remembered *The Lady of Shalott.* She remembered the dingy green school book it came in, called *Narrative Art in Verse.* They had been told that it was a fable of the Victorian middle-class spinster, as her uncle was telling her now.

9

'She wasn't even meant to go to the window and see who passed by,' said Irene sadly. 'Why don't you think it's a good poem?'

Her uncle spread his hands wide. 'You don't have to take my judgement as final. I suppose Tennyson wasn't very fashionable when I was young.'

'I hardly remember the words,' she said, 'only, it seems so true to my life, cut off from the ordinary everyday life of other people. What I hate most is the idea that we cripples would be happier if we never saw or envied normal people – like that holiday camp I got sent to last summer with the wheel-chair races and all that nightmarish well-meaning jollity.'

'Yet you admit some people enjoyed it,' he said.

'Because it's the only holiday they ever get,' she objected. 'If they had the chance they'd enjoy going to Butlins with a party of able-bodied people a great deal more.'

'*You* wouldn't enjoy Butlins,' he said. 'That's "the ordinary life in the ordinary world" which you say you want, but you'd find it as hateful as hospital.'

'I daresay I wouldn't enjoy Butlins,' she admitted, 'but that isn't the point I'm trying to make. It may sound bitter, but I believe ordinary healthy people don't want to see us when they're having a good time, so they kid themselves it's better for us not to see and envy them. So all we are offered is the ghetto holiday camp where we can be all-cripples-together.'

'Do you call a hospital a ghetto too?' he asked. 'Or does it make it a little more bearable that there are practical reasons for segregating you like this?'

'I don't know,' she said unhappily. He did not know how miserable she was, how close to tears, until she suddenly burst out, 'Oh, Uncle William, why did I ever agree to come? How can I survive another five weeks here?'

Uncle William could never cope with raw emotion and even as she spoke she wished she could have withdrawn her outburst. Then they could have made jokes about life in hospital and he would have talked so wittily that even the grotesque and piteous things would have seemed comic. Instead, here she was, weeping helplessly, and her uncle equally helpless to comfort her.

'Dear little Irene,' he said. 'Why won't you let me send you those bottles of champagne?'

The absurdity of it! If she had not been weeping she would have burst out laughing, but as it was it only made her sob the more.

'You've no idea the effect it would have on your spirits,' he said, patting her hand.

'You don't understand. I couldn't drink champagne here in Granstead.'

'But I'll talk to Sister . . .'

'It's not that. It's . . . well, everyone is so poor.'

'And you don't want them to think you're rich.'

'I daresay by your standards I'm not rich,' said Irene. Her uncle's attitude to money always irritated her; he could dispose of cases of champagne and yet believe that the big divide between poverty and riches was a thing of the past. 'I don't know how I dare to complain of my lot when other people are so much worse off. But somehow knowing that doesn't help.'

'No one is poor nowadays,' he said cheerfully – the very thing calculated to annoy her.

'You can't guess what it's like when there's no longer an earner in the family,' she said heatedly. 'Whenever I come into hospital I realize just how lucky I am, just how well off we are. There are some people for whom this place is a treat, an unaccustomed luxury. People who dread going home.'

'You owe it to your mother's devotion, not to riches,' he said.

'It's money too,' she insisted. She thought, for instance, of Janice. Janice was nearest to her in age in the ward, being twenty-six. Irene was eighteen, all the others elderly. Janice was a sweet girl and often came to talk to Irene because she felt she must be lonely among all those old people. Whatever they might start talking about, it always came back to the same theme. Janice had started rheumatoid arthritis when her first baby was born. Now she had two toddlers and it was becoming increasingly difficult for her to cope. Her husband did everything for her, 'Just as my mother does for me,' she explained to her uncle. 'He's just as devoted, but he's got a job as well – a good job, but he's thinking of giving it up to look after his wife and children. They can't go on as they are, and yet if he gives up work they won't be able to pay the mortgage and the hire purchase, they'll have to give up the car which enables her to go out sometimes. The doctor has only sent her into hospital to give her a rest and time to think, so that they can decide what to do.'

'She must have a mother or mother-in-law,' said her uncle, cheerful and disbelieving.

'Her own mother is an invalid,' said Irene indignantly, 'and they'd have to give up the bungalow and find somewhere to live in London without stairs to be near the mother-in-law.'

Still unperturbed, her uncle pointed out that the mother-in-law could move.

'You expect her father-in-law to find a new job in a new place at fifty? He's been working for the same firm for thirty years.' She knew she had not convinced her uncle, but she was relieved when he changed the conversation. It was a subject on which it was pointless to argue with him.

'I've brought you some books,' he said. 'Don't tell me you can't read poetry in hospital.'

Irene laughed. 'One of the nurses picked up the last book you lent me. She took one look and raised her eyes to heaven. Just imagine her expression when she finds it's poetry this time.'

'May as well be hanged for a sheep as for a lamb,' he said. 'Anyway, I'm recommending it for purely practical reasons. I know your hands aren't strong enough to hold a heavy book. You were complaining of the pain in them with having to lie still such long hours. You said you'd have to give up reading once you were in bed. So I thought, poetry. The whole point of poetry is that you should read it over and over again, which saves a lot of page turning. When your hands are tired you can drop the book and ponder, without wondering what is going to happen next. Prose moves in a straight line and you have to follow it to the end, while poetry crystallizes round a point. Also, it comes in slim volumes.'

'You really are thoughtful,' she said, 'thank you. They're sure to move me into a lower bed as soon as one is available – Sister promised. But I'll read poetry until then.'

'I suppose you can't get away from the television when you're stuck in bed,' he said. 'Do they have it on all the time?'

'It's supposed to be silent,' she said. 'You listen on the headphones. After all, it's a blessing for most patients so I can't really complain. You don't realize how extraordinary it is to want to read – let alone to read poetry.'

'You must dare to be extraordinary,' he said. 'I'll never come and see you again if you decide you've got to be just like everyone else.'

'You don't realize how difficult it is in hospital if you don't fit in with everyone else,' she said sadly. 'It's this compulsory life in common. All the same, I promise to read your books. I tell you what – do you think you could find me *The Lady of Shalott*? In a slim volume, of course. I've taken a sudden fancy to reading it again.'

The other patients were just beginning to come back from occupational therapy. The brief privacy they had enjoyed was over. Visitors weren't supposed to come during occupational therapy. Sister thought OT was very important and would never agree to let patients give it a miss, though you couldn't help suspecting that this was just because she had a tidy mind and did not like one or two people left behind in the ward. But Uncle William was an exception: she would allow him anything. No one would have suspected that Sister would be so susceptible to male charm – but, then, so few males had ever dared try.

The full convoy arrived, some wheeled by nurses, others walking with sticks and crutches.

'Playing truant again! Got your boyfriend visiting, I see, I see,' cried out the woman from the bed next to Irene's. This was Mrs Boundy. She supposed there was something witty in pretending she thought Uncle William was a boyfriend.

Although nearly sixty she behaved in an arch, provocative manner to any man who appeared on the scene. Her frizzy hair was imperfectly dyed and every morning she spent at least half an hour putting on her war-paint, a thick layer not quite bridging the furrows. She had no visitors of her own, so she always tried to buttonhole other people's. Now she moved in on Uncle William; had he come far, where did he come from? Oh, but he must know so-and-so then, an old, old friend of Mrs Boundy's. Wanted to marry her once, but she had already met her Boundy then, although he was away at the war. Everyone had once wanted to marry Mrs Boundy, if you believed what she said. Odd that none of them came to visit her, thought Irene bitterly. Mrs Boundy had a monstrous wink which contorted every muscle in her face. She would lean forward, thrust her face into yours, and then produce this extraordinary grimace. Uncle William was somewhat taken aback.

Irene was growing desperate. There were important things she wanted to say to her uncle and now she had lost her opportunity. Soon they would come to put her to bed and he would have to leave. If only this dreadful woman would leave them alone. 'Do have one,' she said, thrusting a box of chocolates at Mrs Boundy, 'and give one to everyone else.'

'Oo, I say, this is generous,' cried Mrs Boundy. She spent an unconscionable time choosing a chocolate for herself. 'Mr Boundy never could abide what he called the browny ones – you know, coffee and caramel and truffle. He always left them for me. They were my favourites – like "Jack Spratt could eat no fat, his wife could eat no lean".' She went off into peals of laughter at her own wit, and departed at last with the box of chocolates.

'Uncle William,' said Irene hurriedly, 'if you love me at all, do try to persuade my mother to go away. I'm sorry I cried. Don't tell her that, will you? Tell her I'm quite contented. And don't make her think I want to get rid of her, because anyway I don't. Just say I'd be much happier if I thought she was having a good time. She's always talking about going to see Rose. Why can't she go now?'

'I'll do my best,' said her uncle, 'but you know how she loves to be indispensable, so I can't promise I'll succeed in persuading her she's not needed. I don't know what she'd do without you! You know, you did her a good turn by becoming a permanent invalid.'

You made a slip then, thought Irene. You said permanent, instead of keeping up the pretence that I'm going to get better. Aloud she said, 'That's unkind. Mother never wanted me to be ill. You seem to forget she's growing old. She needs a break and I wish she'd take one. When Dr Roberts suggested I should come in here, she jumped at the opportunity of getting me out of the house. So why can't she go away?'

'It shall be arranged,' said her uncle. 'You can rely on me.'

Chapter II

I DON'T suppose he'll persuade her to go away, thought Irene. She felt defeated. The first few days in hospital had reduced her to her lowest ebb. She told herself that once she got used to it, it would become bearable. Everyone went out of their way to be kind to her because she was so much younger than the others — but still she loathed it. She could only see five weeks spreading before her, each made up of minutes, hours, days, all as agonizing as the first ones. To think that she had come into hospital voluntarily! Dr Roberts had left her free to choose; he had merely recommended a course of hydrotherapy to limber her up in preparation for the hip operations he proposed. Irene's mother had jumped at the suggestion. At the time Irene had tried to drive a bargain — 'You *will* go away on holiday if I go into hospital?' she had said.

Irene was not an only child but her sisters had been in their teens when she was born, so by the time she became ill they had long since left home. For the past six years she had been the central preoccupation of her mother's life and in those years she had become totally dependent on her. There had been a period, two or three years earlier, when she had seemed to be improving, but then her hip joints had collapsed; since then it had been a long, gradual defeat. Little by little she became unable to look after herself. She could still walk, if only in slow motion, and she had always refused to have a wheelchair in the house. It fidgeted her mother, who would have found it far more convenient to push her where she was wanted, instead of waiting for her to come; but she understood why Irene insisted on battling on, knowing that once she stopped moving she would lose the power to move. When Irene's condition flared up and she was in pain, her mother could not bear to see her struggling to do things which could so easily be done for her. For pity's sake, she would step in and undo the buttons, or dress her. At such times Irene perhaps still had the strength of will to struggle on, but not the extra strength to fight for the right to do things for herself. There would be terrible hysterical scenes between the two of them, when Irene, exhausted and desperate, would rail at the mother who did everything for her.

Irene knew they needed a rest from each other; they were too closely knotted together; and the only way she could give her mother a rest was by consenting to go into hospital. Now it seemed her mother had no intention of going away. It was a splendid opportunity to redecorate Irene's room and, anyway, how could she go abroad and leave poor little Irene unvisited in hospital? Anything Irene said sounded like ingratitude.

She lay crying helplessly, all because her mother would not go away. It was stupid, she knew, and in a moment somebody would notice and would want to know what was the matter and she would have nothing to tell them. She was already in bed and she had too little movement in her hips to sit up, but she could turn on her side and look out of the window. In that way, perhaps her tears would pass unnoticed. The television was on now, so nobody bothered her. It was supposed to be silent but there was always a murmur from the screen, something you might not notice if you were busy and occupied, but which forced itself upon you if you lay idle. Faintly but unmistakably she could hear the voice of a typical housewife failing to sound convincingly amazed by the whiteness of her wash, followed by the false enthusiasm of the hired salesman.

Something still nagged at the back of her mind, a disappointment whose cause she had forgotten. Then she remembered: her uncle had said *permanent* invalid. He did not believe, no one believed, in the bright future the specialist promised her – that the hip operations would give her movement, freedom from pain, a new life. Of course she had never wholly believed it herself. She knew Dr Roberts never told you the worst – that was his policy. But did her uncle (and all the others) really think there was no hope for her? That the operations would not make an appreciable difference? Had she let herself be deceived with empty promises?

At home she had been able to forget how much her condition had deteriorated of late, because it had all happened gradually. Coming into hospital had brought her up face to face with the change. It was nearly two years since she had last been in there, and then she had still been able to get about by herself; now she had to depend on help from other people for almost everything she did. The building was old and had not been designed for its present purpose. There were long corridors and everything was as far away as possible. Irene could not even flog all the way to the lavatory by herself; somebody had to take her in a wheel-chair or else, if she was already in bed, they brought a bed pan. Irene found this the ultimate humiliation; she was not ill – no iller than she had been at home – but she had become a helpless invalid.

So her uncle did not believe she could ever be any better . . .

It was too easy to surrender to despair. With a conscious effort Irene pushed the temptation away, because if she allowed herself to lose hope then, indeed, she could not get better. No operation would cure her if she lost the will to be whole and healthy. She thought of the book her uncle had leant her, the book which had raised the nurse's eyebrows. It was about an imaginary country called *Erewhon* where they held that illness was a self-chosen offence and crime a misfortune in need of a cure, so they sent the sick to prison and the criminals to hospital. Oddly enough, this idea had filled Irene with hope, because, if she had chosen to be ill, surely she could change her fate once more. She was quite prepared to believe that she had chosen to be ill, subconsciously, once upon a time. She had been a quiet child, her nose always in a book, who had hated games and the outdoor life that her mother was so keen on. It had always seemed a great luxury to be ill enough to be excused games and left indoors to read the books that she liked – which were not the books that she ought to be reading to get through the exams; for though she seemed studious, Irene had never excelled at school work and she dreaded exams.

Now, how she would have welcomed them in exchange for being ill! But how could her conscious mind change her unconscious mind? How could she reverse the process she had started all those years ago? She lay thinking, wondering: she had escaped from those earlier things, but was she perhaps still trying to escape, refusing to accept the whole of life as it was offered to her? Hospital, for instance. That last time she had been in, she had still been independent and so she had been able to be self-sufficient; she had needed nothing from anyone and had kept herself to herself. But now she had to rely on others and so she had to collaborate. Looking back, she was amazed at the way she had managed to ignore everyone. This time, after two or three days, she knew more about the nurses than she had learnt in all her stay before. There was Eileen, who had been so astounded at her choice of reading matter; Eileen was very little older than Irene and she had assumed straight away that Irene was longing for company of her own age, so she had told her about the singers and film stars she admired, the discotheque where she went dancing and the young man she hoped would take her out. Irene's life did not contain boyfriends and discotheques, but she was grateful for the kindness that prompted these confidences.

I must accept hospital, thought Irene. I must not turn my back on it, shut it out, count the days to my release. That means that I must accept Sister too, she thought with a sigh. After all, Sister had appeared very reasonable and considerate when she had come to talk to her about the bed. It just happened that there were a limited number of low beds and by some strange chance there were a lot of patients with short legs in hospital just at the moment. Irene caught herself in the act of blaming Dr Roberts for sending her into hospital just when there wasn't a low bed and she laughed at herself, because how could the poor man be expected to know the length of the legs of all the patients in Granstead? She must accept him too; after all, some of the patients did not want to hear the worst, they did not want to be told that the doctor was not all-wise. They preferred unbelievable promises. She had heard them complaining of the surgeon, Mr Harris, because he had said he could not guarantee the success of his work. 'Why do he do these operations then, if he's not sure?' someone had asked.

What else should she accept? thought Irene. Her mother? Didn't she spend her whole time fighting to accept her? Mrs Boundy? Poor old goose, she had probably had a hard life. Thinking of the other old ladies in the ward, Irene's mind came to rest gratefully on the thought of Mrs Sparrow, or Birdie, as everyone called her. Even last time, when she had been so independent, she had come to love old Birdie. She was the only person Irene had met in hospital to whom she could really talk. What luck they were in together this time.

Irene turned over to look round the ward. Birdie was over in her corner. She was talking to Mavis. Mavis wasn't one of the patients; she worked down in the pool. She wasn't a physio-therapist, nor yet a nurse – nothing as grand as that. She was only a menial. Mavis had worked there since the pool was first built and she knew everyone who ever came for treatment. In some ways she knew a great deal more than the trained staff. She always undressed and dressed the patients when they came for hydrotherapy and she knew by some instinct how to move their limbs when taking off their clothes, although no one had pain in exactly the same place. The qualified physiotherapists would sometimes seize a foot and jerk it in some impossible direction – they did not necessarily understand bodies just because they had been taught all about them. But Mavis did. With her huge ungainly gentle hands she would move joints that always caught when other people tried to manipulate them; she would move them past the invisible ratchet and you would never feel her doing it.

Mavis had not come up to the ward in pursuit of duty. It was time for her to go home but she had just slipped up to see Birdie and to give her the wool she had bought for her in town. As Granstead was a hospital to which the same people came back again and again, it was more human – if also more exasperating – than most hospitals. The staff knew the patients of old and patients always addressed nurses by their Christian names, even though Sister tried to insist on the more formal title of 'nurse'. Birdie had been coming to Granstead as long as Mavis had worked there. Irene lay and watched them. They were only talking about knitting patterns, but it had the warmth of real life.

Before she left, Mavis came over and spoke to Irene. 'In bed already, dearie?' she said.

'They've put me in this great huge bed. I can't get in by myself,' said Irene.

'What did they do a thing like that for?' said Mavis.

'It can't be helped,' said Irene. 'There aren't any others.'

'Poor little Ireen,' said Mavis, raising her big ungainly hands as if she would at that moment have put matters right. She was a big rawboned woman and could lift Irene singlehanded. But she was going home now. 'It's a long time to lie there thinking. Shall I give you those 'ere headphones of yours?'

Irene said no. 'I like to watch out of the window as the light goes golden and then rusty. I like to watch that little wood out there and all the people who come out in the evening to take the air.'

Mavis gazed uncomprehendingly out of the window. 'That little wood?' she asked, puzzled.

'Yes,' said Irene. 'You see where I mean – that little lane goes into it. I often wonder where it goes.'

'That there ain't no wood,' said Mavis.

'Well, what would you call it then?'

Mavis considered a definition. 'It's just some trees,' she said.

'What's the difference?' asked Irene, inwardly amused. 'A wood's just some trees.'

'That there ain't no wood,' said Mavis obstinately. 'I'll tell you where that lane goes, too – it goes to Glebe Farm and Glebe Cottage, and that there is where I live. You keep your eyes skinned and you'll see me go past on me bike. I'll give you a wave. What d'you think of that? See that gate up under the big beech tree? That's where I'll stop and wave to you.'

The idea of Mavis disappearing into the picture was almost unimaginable. 'Do do that, Mavis,' said Irene. 'Please.'

Mavis, still staring out of the window, commented, 'There goes Miss Harriet. She's off to see the inventor, I'll be bound. She do spend a lot of time down the Glebe these days.' One of the little thumb-sized figures was strolling along the lane. In the still, golden evening light she looked curiously close, as if you had only to call to her and she would turn her head. Yet in between them stretched the hospital outbuildings and the great expanse of the hundred-acre beet field.

'I'll keep watching till I see you wave,' said Irene.

As she lay waiting – and it seemed to take Mavis an interminable time to reach the point where she entered the picture – Irene thought of the Lady of Shalott. That curse – she remembered – didn't the mirror break when she went to the window? Would something catastrophic like that happen when Mavis waved, when communication was established between the real world and the world of fantasy?

Suddenly – she seemed to have appeared without approaching, as if there had been a cut in the film – Mavis was there waving. She had got off her bike and she moved her arm in long slow rhythmic sweeps above her head. Irene would have liked to make some answering signal. If she could have raised her arm vertically it was just possible Mavis could have seen it, but she could not raise her arm like that. Sometimes, when she was tired, she had to raise one elbow with the other hand in order to bring a cup to her lips – there was so little strength in her arms. So there could be no two-way communication.

Mavis expected no answering signal. She continued her slow unexcited semaphore and Irene wondered if she was counting fifty or a hundred. Then another figure appeared beside her. Mavis stopped waving. They spoke. Irene could see that Mavis pointed over to the hospital. But Miss Harriet – Irene could not be sure if it was the same figure or not, but that was the only name she knew to attach to the people out there – Miss Harriet did not follow her gesture to look over towards the hospital. Mavis was telling her something about Irene but she wasn't interested. Irene felt a wave of disillusionment go over her; she did not want people out there to be told about her. She had intended to watch Mavis disappear into the mouth of the wood that was not a wood, but instead she turned over and slowly edged her hand across the locker and performed the complicated manoeuvre of disengaging one of her uncle's books from the chocolate box and the fruit basket, pill bottles and vase of flowers, biscuit tin and water jug. She would see what he had brought her this time.

Chapter III

☙

IRENE'S mother drove a half-timbered Morris Minor. It was nice and roomy for the dogs, her Airedales, Pax and Tony. Mrs Paxton took care to park the car in the shade. She spoke authoritatively to the dogs: they were to stay there and keep quiet. They had raised their heads half expectantly when she drew up, but dropped them meekly again. Mrs Paxton stood no nonsense from her dogs. She had a very low opinion of people who could not control their pets – or their children; it was so easy, after all, if you started off as you meant to go on. Mrs Paxton used to breed dogs, but she had had to give that up as Irene grew more dependent on her. There were many things she had had to give up and some of them Irene did not even guess. Her mother had developed quite a taste for giving things up, but she was not ostentatious about it.

She gathered together her baskets and strode rapidly towards the hospital. She was a tall woman and athletic-looking, despite her sixty-odd years. Whatever she was doing, be it calling on the neighbours or digging the vegetable garden, she always wore the same clothes: brown corduroy slacks, a sailcloth slop, ankle socks and schoolgirl sandals, or else wellingtons in muddy weather. She belonged to the generation which had first rebelled against hats and the most she would allow herself was a headscarf; today her grey bobbed hair was uncovered.

'What a lot you've brought,' said Irene, not entirely grateful when she observed the posse of baskets that her mother had parked on the floor before embracing her. 'My locker is already full.'

'I'll ask Sister to put it all on one side for you. There's another consignment of muesli and a big kilner jar of black currant purée – that'll have to go in the fridge. Plenty of apples, too, our own apples – the first Worcesters. And I've brought some carrots, because I know how you like raw carrots. I've done some baking too, your favourite date and walnut buns . . .'

The catalogue went on and on, giving Irene time to relax herself forcibly and tell herself it was no good protesting; she would never change her mother, so she had much better put a pleased face on it. Not that she did not like all the special healthy foods her mother believed in – in fact she much preferred to eat them than the baked beans and flabby thin sliced bread the hospital provided; it was just – well, none of the staff had ever complained or said it gave extra trouble, but she always felt apologetic about being made different from the others. She hated being made an exception of. She was shamed and embarrassed by her mother's assumption that she was a special case with a right to special privileges.

'I brought such a lot because, well – I've got something to tell you.' Mrs Paxton drew her chair close to Irene's, took her hand and gazed into her eyes. 'Your father's been pressing me and Uncle William's been assuring me that now you're settled in here you're really quite happy and comfortable, so, dearest, I rang up Rose last night . . . they insisted I should . . .'

'But mother, how splendid! You're actually going to Italy?'

Mrs Paxton's brow cleared. 'I knew you'd take it like that! You're so brave, so unselfish, my own sweet Irene. It is my one chance, you see. Once they start on these operations I shan't be able to leave the country – no, of course I couldn't leave you if it was touch and go whether you were improving or . . . it's just that so many things can happen after an operation, I couldn't possibly leave you with an easy mind. But now I feel you're in safe hands and Dr Roberts wanted you to stay in for five weeks, so they won't suddenly decide to throw you out. Rose is up at the villa on the Lago Maggiore. I wouldn't be nearly so tempted if it was just their flat in Milan. Just think of it – I may even get some sailing!'

'You must write and tell me what it's like,' said Irene. 'I

shall look forward to your letters.' She must not sound too jubilant.

'Poor little Irene – I feel a beast going away like this and telling you all about it, when you can't come too.'

'But mother, I don't want everyone else to be miserable just because I'm . . . in hospital' – not miserable, which was what she had been going to say. 'I shall enjoy reading your letters and knowing that you're having a good time.'

'We'll take you to Italy, my pet, when you've had the operations. Not to that dreadful flat in Milan, up all those stairs. I'm longing to see what the villa is like.'

'But I shall be able to go up stairs when I've had the operations,' said Irene, insisting on the bright make-believe future. 'I want to go to Milan, to see the Brera and the Last Supper and everything.'

'You shall go with William, then. The two of you can go to as many museums as you like. But dear me! Rose says I've even got to take some "good clothes" to the villa. I should've thought you could've worn what you liked in the country. Italians are so dressy, she says.'

'You mustn't shame her,' said Irene. She thought of her sister, whom she hardly knew. It was more like having an aunt, except that Rose complained to her of their mother as only daughters complain. Rose had always seemed middle-aged to her, though even now she was not yet forty. But she was one of those formal people who always wear stockings and never sit on the floor, and insist on table napkins and butter knives. Most summers she came with her children, whom her mother thought unhealthy because they were sallow and tiresome because they were afraid of dogs – children who were never allowed to get their clothes dirty. Mrs Paxton was sorry for them: children should be allowed to romp around. She did not really believe that Rose had found a childhood of aertex shirts little short of torture.

Every Christmas and birthday Rose sent her sister beautiful hand-embroidered nighties; every time she wrote an accompanying apology, begging Irene to tell her if there was anything she would rather have. But Irene was grateful for the nighties, knowing that if it had been left to her mother she would have gone to hospital in boys' pyjamas. Irene liked pretty things.

'You mustn't let Rose down,' she said.

'I don't know why Rose bothers so much about what people think. I don't care if Italians are dressy. I don't see why I should have to be dressy too. I've always told Rose that what we are is more important than what we wear.' Just then a nurse came by and Mrs Paxton took the opportunity to hand over the contents of the baskets, with long complex instructions of how they were to be stored and when eaten.

'That jar'll have to have a label with Ireen's name on it or we won't know who it belongs to,' said the nurse. In hospital Irene was always called 'Ireen', an error of pronunciation Mrs Paxton never failed to correct.

'If you could just find me a bit of sellotape I'll write a label,' she said. 'And, you know, the name is Iren-e. You sound the final "e". Such a pretty name, don't you think? You mustn't pronounce it Ireen as if it rhymed with Eileen.'

'Eileen is a pretty name too,' said Irene attempting to catch the nurse's eye. How many times had she warned her mother that some people were called Eileen and she mustn't speak the name in that tone of disdain, however much she disliked it herself? But nothing stirred in Mrs Paxton's memory and she breezed on giving orders and instructions to this unaccountably surly nurse. Even when the nurse had gone, and Irene told her she was called Eileen, she just remarked, 'I put my foot in it, did I? Well, it can't be helped.'

She'll say exactly the same thing next time, thought Irene. She felt an immense relief that her mother was going away. For the rest of the visit she attempted to be bright and asked endless questions about Rose and the villa, what was to become of the dogs and her father, but all the time she was longing for it to be over. Mrs Paxton was difficult to dislodge. Even when the nurses came to put Irene to bed she did not leave, but spent a long time closeted with Sister. Then she came back to say her last farewells.

27

There was little more to say except to repeat what had been said before. But Mrs Paxton felt guilty about leaving. It would be a month before she saw her daughter again.

'You will write?' Irene urged her. Then, looking for an excuse to send her away, she asked, 'Have you brought Pax and Tony with you?'

'I hope the car is still in the shade,' said her mother, glad also of the excuse to leave. 'I promised to give them a walk.'

'Mother,' said Irene, 'look out of the window. Do you see that little wood and the lane that leads into it? It can't be private because I see all sorts of people going along it. Do you think you could find your way there? I want to see you walking with the dogs, as we're saying goodbye for so long. It would please me so much.'

Her mother was touched. It had been just the right word to say, the right note to part on. Irene lay and waited. Again, it seemed a long time. At last they appeared within the picture, her mother and the dogs. She saw her mother stop, shade her eyes and gaze across at the hospital, a tiny remote figure. In that moment her heart smote her and she loved her mother. She was filled with an aching regret that they had not talked properly, that they never did speak heart to heart without fictions and misunderstandings. She was glad, too, with a sudden joy, that her mother had proved herself a free agent, not a mere pawn in the psychological game of needing to be needed. One free action had broken the closed circuit and filled the future with infinite new possibilities.

Chapter IV

Before she went abroad Mrs Paxton rang up one of Irene's friends and urged her to visit Irene in hospital. 'Don't tell her I spoke to you,' she said. 'She doesn't like me interfering in her affairs.' She knew Clare had not seen Irene for nearly a year.

Clare felt somewhat daunted at the prospect of visiting Irene in hospital. She had already had a letter from Irene, and her mother had said she ought to go, but without Mrs Paxton's phone call she would probably never have got round to it. She felt guilty; it had happened so often : she was always meaning to go and visit Irene and then she didn't.

Two summers before, Irene had gone on holiday with Clare and her family. At that time her condition had been improving and there had even been talk of sending her back to school; when this came to nothing, Mrs Paxton had arranged the holiday with Clare's family, knowing how disappointed Irene was and how isolated she felt. She could still get about quite easily, but her gait was somewhat awkward because her hip-joints had already begun to collapse. The improvement which had given her so much hope had only been temporary. Until then she had never really thought about the future – present pain had absorbed all her attention; at sixteen she realized she could never get better, only worse. Clare was wrapped up in her own affairs. She wanted to leave school, while her parents insisted that she should stay on to do A levels. She talked about this incessantly – Irene's tragedy was unreal to her, or perhaps too appalling for her to grasp. Despite the daily company of her friend Irene felt desperately lonely, shut off in a private nightmare which no one could share.

Since then the two friends had seen less and less of one

another. Clare had stayed on at school, but her life had been filled with new activities and new friends; the only new things in Irene's life came out of books. So Clare was glad when another friend volunteered to go with her. It was, anyway, a tiresome cross-country journey with a change of buses, so it was good to have company. All the effort seemed worthwhile when they saw Irene's face of pleasure and astonishment at their arrival.

Yet, after the first greetings, it was difficult to think of anything to say. Clare and Diana reminded each other of things they could tell her that had happened at school. It all seemed very remote to Irene, but her interest was kindled when Clare began to talk of her plans for the future. She was going up to London to do a course in speech therapy. At the holiday camp for cripples there had been some who suffered from speech difficulties; Irene had hated seeing them patronized and talked down to as if they were idiots, when it was only the articulation of words that caused them difficulty, not the thought behind the words. As a cripple she often found herself treated as an imbecile, so she knew the humiliation of it, and she felt she must make Clare understand. She was not aware how preachy she sounded.

Diana soon lost interest. She was laughing at the silent mouthing figures on the television screen. Irene invited her to take the headphones and Diana hastily turned her back on the screen.

'I wanted to get a flat with some friends,' said Clare. 'But Mummy insists on my going to this hostel. It's not going to be much fun being in London if I have to get in by eleven every night. And, do you know, they don't let you have men in your room after eight o'clock!'

'I ask you!' said Diana. 'If you want to do that sort of thing you can do it at any time of the day.'

'Why do parents go on behaving as if you're a child long after you're grown up?' complained Clare.

'Never mind,' said Irene. 'It's only for a little while. You'll get a job. You'll get married. Then you'll be independent.

You'll even have children of your own to treat like children.'

'You sound like a school-ma'am,' said Diana.

The reproof hurt Irene. She looked at her life and theirs – how could they seriously complain? 'I only meant that I shall be treated as a child as long as I live. We're all treated like children here. And I shall always be dependent on my mother, or someone else. When my mother takes me out in the wheelchair, people talk to her over my head, as if I weren't there. They even talk about me. It's the sort of thing you do when there's a small child in a push-chair.'

'They must be daft!' Clare exclaimed hurriedly. It sounded too awful. They could talk without being overheard as Mrs Boundy had moved away to talk to somebody else's visitor in a loud voice, but nevertheless Clare lowered her voice to say, after a quick glance round the ward, 'It's like an old people's home. Isn't there anyone else who's young?'

'Janice is young,' Irene said, indicating her with her eyes.

'It must be depressing,' said Clare.

'It is depressing,' said Irene flatly. Why should she gloss over the facts to make them happier?

'It's only for a little while,' said Diana, triumphantly paying her back in her own coin.

'Oh, shut up,' said Clare, for which Irene was grateful.

'Some of them are splendid people,' she said ' – it's not just because they're old. It's because they're "recidivists". Did you ever read *Erewhon*?'

Diana replied defensively, 'We're brainless – we don't read books.'

'It's about an imaginary country,' Irene went on, 'where everything is topsy-turvy – they put sick people in prison because they think it's your fault that you're ill, and they send criminals to hospital because they think it's something they can't help but could be cured of. That's why I called them recidivists – you know, the old lags who come back to prison again and again. They feel lost in the world outside and they almost enjoy the security of prison, just as some patients here enjoy the comforts, being looked after, cups of tea brought to them, and the company, of course. I suppose I'm afraid of becoming a recidivist like the rest of them and that's what makes it so depressing.'

Clare said, 'But they can't get better just by wanting to. Whereas someone can stop stealing or committing crimes.'

'Can they?' said Irene. 'I'm not so sure it's as simple as that. I believe if there really were a new wonder cure for arthritis it wouldn't work on some people because they're no longer willing to change their whole lives and be well. They're not ready to start back at square one, looking after themselves. They'd rather sit in front of the everlasting telly waiting for the next cup of tea to be brought.'

'I don't see why you should grudge them the television,' said Diana.

Irene sighed. So she'd done just what she wanted to avoid – she had criticized and condemned her fellow patients, and Diana, who would walk out of the ward free and need never come back, could blandly stick up for them and be right – because of course she was right; why shouldn't they watch television?

Clare at least tried to sympathize. 'Poor Irene,' she said, 'You must be lonely here with all these old ladies. Does anyone come to see you now your mother's gone away? If only we lived a bit closer!'

'I tell you who lives in Granstead,' said Diana, ' – that's Hatty Moss.'

'D'you remember Hatty Moss?' Clare asked Irene. 'In the form below us? Perhaps she was after your time. She was Portia in the school play. She always was good at acting. She won the verse speaking competition when she was ever so small and she would have won it every year only they decided that wasn't fair on other people.'

Clare and Diana began to reminisce about this girl, but Irene wasn't really listening. Ever since Clare had said, 'Now your mother's gone away' she had gone off on a track of her own.

How did Clare know? She jumped to the conclusion that her mother had rung Clare and asked her to come. She hadn't come of her own accord.

'She's frightfully stuck up,' Diana was saying. 'She doesn't care to mix with ordinary mortals like us. We don't understand her great poetic soul.'

'She's just shy, that's all,' said Clare. 'Would you like us to go and call on Hatty?' she asked Irene. 'We could tell her about you and then she could come and see you.'

'But I don't even know her,' said Irene.

'She's really very nice and it would be someone of your own age,' said Clare.

'I don't want people to come and see me out of charity,' Irene said bitterly. 'I'm quite all right as I am.'

Afterwards, when they had gone, it occurred to her that Clare would have rung up her mother anyway if she had been planning to come to the hospital, if only so that their visits should not coincide; there was no reason to assume that she had come at her mother's request. She felt sorry that she had been so hard on them. Just before they left Clare had said, 'Why, you never unwrapped your parcel.' She had not opened it because she could not; her hands had not the strength to tear the fancy paper, let alone the sellotape, but she felt embarrassed for their sakes so that when Clare mentioned it she did attempt to scrabble at the wrappings with her crooked fingers.

'Let me help you,' said Clare. It was the first time that afternoon that she had really noticed how crippled Irene was, and she was horrified. 'Your hands never used to be like that,' she said helplessly. 'We must try and come again.'

Irene saw the look of distress in her eyes. She knew that she was longing to be reassured, to be told it was not as bad as it looked, to be told that she could help by coming again; but she gave her no encouragement or reassurance. Why should I have to soften the blow for her, she thought. Is this world really so different from *Erewhon*? People are embarrassed by illness, they don't want to know about it, and as for us who are unfortunate enough to be sick, they expect us to keep quiet about it and conceal it as far as possible for fear it should cause them distress.

But afterwards she was sorry she had not found a kind word to say to Clare, that she had not encouraged her to think that another visit would be welcome.

Chapter V

THE specialists and the surgeon came down from London on Thursdays to visit their patients in Granstead hospital, and so it was usually the following day that those whom they discharged left the hospital. Irene had been hoping, indeed expecting, that a low bed would fall vacant; Eileen broke the bad news to her.

'There was only one,' she said, 'and Sister says Mrs Rawson's to have it.'

'It was Eileen's fault,' said the other nurse who was helping to lift her off the bed. 'Sister don't like to be told. Eileen ought to have known, but the great booby bursts out about your wanting a lower bed and so of course Sister has to decide to give it to someone else. "Mrs Rawson has been waiting longer," she says, all hoity-toity, just to let us know she's running this ward, not us.'

'I only meant to remind her,' said Eileen. 'I'm awfully sorry. It's true what Linda says, but all the same, if you don't remind her, Sister's quite capable of forgetting.'

Eileen sounded so upset that Linda said, 'You won't blame Eileen, will you? She's kicking herself now. The trouble is, Sister's impossible. You can't ask her anything, 'cos she'll only bite your head off, and you can't tell her anything either. She tells you to do something quite ridiculous and she won't let you tell her that this patient's been doing so-and-so all along. Much better to keep your mouth shut and go on doing what you were going to do anyway.'

'Of course it wasn't your fault,' said Irene to Eileen. 'Has Mrs Rawson been in longer?'

'I thought she came in on Monday, same as you,' said Eileen.

35

'The thing is, I've never heard her say about wanting a lower bed. She's an old lazybones if you ask me – she's quite happy to be lifted about and waited on hand and foot.'

All this went to undermine Irene's resolve to accept the hospital. Why should she accept injustice? Wasn't it better to put up a fight? When Sister came round she was feeling very rebellious.

'I had hoped,' said Sister, 'that we'd have two low beds, one for you and one for Mrs Rawson, but it hasn't turned out that way. I knew you'd understand that I had to offer the only one there was to Mrs Rawson – she has the same difficulty as you and she's been waiting even longer.'

'It's a pity I don't like watching television,' said Irene in a chilly voice. 'It makes such a long time to lie doing nothing.'

'You've read all your books?' asked Sister, sounding most solicitous.

'It's difficult for me to read lying down because of my hands,' said Irene.

When Sister heard about her hands she asked her if she had ever had wax treatment. 'If only you had told me about your hands before,' she said. 'This can easily be arranged and you'll find it gives you a great deal of relief.' When they came back from the pool in the mornings they had a rest and then they went down to the gym to do exercises; instead of doing exercises Irene could have wax baths for her hands down in physiotherapy.

Sister was really pleased to have been able to do something for little Miss Paxton. Poor child, she thought – so young and already so badly crippled. But Irene found it hard to be grateful as she felt all the time that Sister had cheated her of the low bed; wax baths would hardly make up for the long hours spent abed and the misery of being so dependent upon other people. It was that afternoon that her mother came, but Irene said nothing to her about the bed; it would never do to let her see how difficult things were in hospital or she would feel bad about going away. Bottling up her grievances made Irene feel even more rebellious.

36

There was no treatment at the weekends but on Monday morning Irene should have gone down to the pool. The physiotherapist came up to the ward to round up the patients and told her she was not on the list for hydrotherapy that week. It seemed as if the whole world was against her. 'What do you mean, I'm not on the list?' she asked indignantly. 'The only reason I was sent into hospital was so's I could have hydrotherapy. It's just a waste of public money to keep me here if I'm not having treatment.'

'It's probably just a clerical error,' said the physiotherapist. She used a soothing tone as if she were dealing with someone totally unreasonable. 'I see you've been put down for wax treatment, so probably someone thought that meant you weren't to have hydrotherapy any longer.'

'Well, Mrs Chandler, if it's just a clerical error I can go down with the others because you know I'm meant to be there.' Irene used too high-handed a tone, calculated, in its turn, to cause annoyance.

'I'll have a word with Miss Howell,' said Mrs Chandler. 'You know she's a great stickler for rules, but we can probably get you back on the list in a day or two.'

'In a day or two!' exclaimed Irene. But Mrs Chandler was already out of the room.

'You got her narked, love,' said Birdie who was on her way out. 'It'll be all right. Just you wait and see.'

Left alone Irene wondered why she had been so stupid as to lose her temper. Her excuse was that she was very tired. She did not sleep well in hospital. She had lain too long in bed and was stiff and painful by the time they finally turned off the television and closed down for the night. In the restless silence and half darkness she lay unrelaxed; towards morning she had dozed off just in time to be woken up for the new day. By then she was so stiff that she wondered if she would ever move again. Now she couldn't even go to the pool, the one form of exercise that was allowed her in hospital.

She was alone in the ward. I should be pleased, she reflected; I'm always longing to be alone. But she was quite incapable of relishing her solitude at that moment. They did not even treat her like a human being. She had been reduced to a name on a list. A typist skipped a line and she lost several days out of her life. She had been sitting fuming for some time when she heard someone enter the ward.

'Hullo love, I was expecting you down in the pool.' It was Mavis.

'And I was expecting to go down to the pool.'

'I thought it was just the usual thing.' Mavis never mentioned periods.

'No, they left me off some list.'

'Birdie just told me. Ready?' She was about to lift Irene into a wheelchair.

'What will Miss Howell say?' said Irene.

'It's what you're in hospital for, ain't it?' said Mavis.

Mavis was so sensible and reassuring. When she had taken off her nighty and put her into her costume, she wheeled her out of the changing rooms and passed the canvas cradle of the hoist under her legs and behind her back. The pool was built up higher than the floor level so that those a little more adept than Irene could sit on the edge and swing their legs over into the water. For the others there was the hoist which was operated by electricity. Mavis switched it on and she began to levitate. It always reminded Irene of knights encased in armour being lowered on to horseback in the film of Henry V.

Today, fearing some outcry at her unscheduled appearance, she was particularly conscious of herself as she swung in mid-air. The hoist seemed to move in slow motion. The pool was spread below her. There was a wide shelf on which you could sit, and the deep part where the water came up to your armpits. It had always struck Irene that they were a grotesque sight in the pool, their misshapen bodies all revealed. Now, her senses sharpened by fear, it seemed that she was being lowered into the pit of hell: the rocking water twisted, blew out or telescoped their submerged limbs. The face of Mrs Boundy looked up in full war-paint, her henna hair hidden under a shocking-pink bathing cap covered with rubber flowers.

'So you got in after all,' she bawled. Was it a malicious attempt to draw attention to Irene's arrival? But nobody took any notice. Miss Howell, the main physiotherapist, was standing outside the pool talking to one of the patients in the water. Mrs Chandler was in the water; she was strapping Janice into a harness which would enable her to float on her back and kick out with her legs. As Irene's feet touched the water, she turned, as if fully aware of her impending presence, caught her legs and guided her down into the water. Irene had tensed, as if expecting violence, but the physiotherapist brought her safely to rest, sitting on the underwater shelf, and then unfastened the cradle and slid it out from under her body. She smiled at Irene. She was sorry she had allowed herself to show her annoyance earlier and she would have liked to make up for it.

'Who brought you down? Mavis?' she asked. 'Good for her – let's hope Miss Howell doesn't kick up a fuss.'

Irene sat and swung her legs. The water resisted but also supported them. When she got into rhythm she could feel the pleasure of pushing against the water, while her joints carried no weight. When she got used to the feeling she slid down off the shelf and began to walk about in the water. It was like pushing a wall before you and had all the exhilaration of effort without the inhibiting terror of a sudden pain in the joints. When she was in the pool Irene realized that it was worth coming into hospital; it was just all that sad waste of time in between.

Meanwhile Mrs Chandler was hooking a device on to the rail at the edge of the pool. 'Who's going to try Mr Pollard's new harness?' she called. There were a number of volunteers, but she appeared to ignore them. 'What about you, Ireen?' she said.

Irene immediately noticed that Miss Howell's eyes were upon them. Here it comes, she thought. But instead of referring to the list and Irene's absence from it, Miss Howell said, in rather chilly tones, 'On your head be it. I only warn you it hasn't been properly tested.'

'What does she mean by tested?' said Mrs Chandler in

Irene's ear. 'Who does she think tests most of the equipment we evolve here in the pool? Can you relax?' she went on. 'I've got hold of you, you're quite safe. That's right.' She slipped the harness under Irene's arms and fastened it across her chest.

This harness was of an entirely different design from the old one into which Janice was strapped. It was a very slight affair, deceptively simple. Support came just in the right place. After the first few moments Irene felt perfectly secure, and she could kick out with all that little force she possessed.

'Feel safe?' asked Mrs Chandler.

Miss Howell was still watching them. 'It's more important to be safe than to feel safe,' she said sententiously.

Irene felt a sudden solidarity with Mrs Chandler. It was partly the result of their quarrel – she wanted to show she no longer bore any ill will – but it was also because they were united against Miss Howell. 'Feeling safe is very important too,' she said. 'We cripples don't do things half the time just because we don't feel safe – we're afraid of falling, afraid of sudden pain.'

'We don't call people cripples in Granstead,' said Miss Howell coldly and, considering the subject closed, ignored Irene and the new harness.

'So you tried Mr Pollard's new harness,' said Mavis afterwards, when she was rubbing her down. 'What shall I tell him you said?'

'It's just the job,' said Irene, 'but I'd like a little more support for my head. Who is Mr Pollard?'

'He lives over at the Glebe Farm.'

'In the wood that isn't a wood?'

Mavis nodded.

'He's a physiotherapist?' asked Irene.

'Oh no! He's a patient. But he's an inventor,' she added mysteriously.

On the way out they passed the contingent of male patients waiting to go into the pool. 'Come on you channel-swimmers!' called Mrs Boundy. 'It's nice and warm in there today – thought you'd catch us in the changing rooms, did you? Better luck next time!' And she went off into hoots of girlish laughter. Once they were in the lift she turned her attention to Irene. 'How did you manage to squeeze yourself in, dearie? You have all the luck,' she said. 'I wouldn't have minded having a go in that new harness. Who is this Mr Pollard?'

Nobody answered her and presently they were back in the ward. Eileen and Linda lifted Irene on to her bed so that she could rest for an hour before going down for the wax treatment. She lay and gazed out of the window at the wood that wasn't a wood, where Mavis lived and where the mysterious Mr Pollard lived. What was it Mavis had called him? Oh yes, the inventor. It was he whom Miss Harriet was going to see. Dear, funny Mavis – it was people like her and Birdie who made the hospital tolerable. But what did she mean by insisting that it wasn't a wood out there when you could see quite plainly that it was? Irene felt sleepy after so much exertion and presently she dozed off. In a dream they were taking her somewhere, but she was naked . . . couldn't they stop to put on her clothes, she had them in her hand? . . . But no, what she had in her hand was a book of poetry . . . Now there was nobody there and the wheelchair was running downhill faster and faster . . .

She awoke with a start. Mr Pollard had something to do with the dream. Had they been going to see him?

Chapter VI

'WHAT did I tell you?' said Eileen. 'It's no good asking Sister, that's what I said.'

'Yes, you did,' said Irene. 'All the same, I felt I had to.'

'We can still do what I suggested, you know.'

'I think better not. It would be open defiance now I've asked.'

Irene loathed occupational therapy, which in Granstead hospital at this time consisted largely of the teaching of crafts. She had never been good at handwork and now with her cramped hands she was compelled to spend two afternoons a week making hideous useless objects. At least, that was how it seemed to her. She could not see that for some patients it was a blessing, a break in the routine; she could only see it as an affront to human dignity – free people came into hospital for medical treatment and they were forced to occupy themselves in this humiliating way. 'I should've thought it was fun making those things,' Eileen had said.

'But they're hideous!' Irene exclaimed. 'Would you want to spend all afternoon winding string round nails?' It was this year's craze – they provided you with black-painted pin-board stuck with nails in various configurations, round which you wound coloured string.

'I don't know,' said Eileen. 'I tell you what, though – we could always leave you in the front hall instead of taking you into OT. You could take a book. There's a vending machine for coffee. Lots of patients take their visitors there so nobody would notice you.'

But Irene had insisted on asking Sister if she could stay up on the ward. It was the one time she could read, as she had to spend the evenings in bed. It was also the one time the ward would be quiet; the constant talk and noise was getting her down. Sometimes she put her earphones on without switching them on, but if she then took up her book Mrs Boundy would sing out, 'Don't you like our conversation, dearie?' She tried to explain all this to Sister, but she made no impression. Sister thought that in some hidden way, which Irene could not be expected to understand, OT would do her good. 'You must give it a try,' she said.

'But I have,' said Irene.

'You must try to join in a bit more. Try to understand that we are doing our best for you.'

'How long have I got to try it before I can give it up?' insisted Irene.

But she met with a flat refusal. 'All patients go to occupational therapy. I don't see that I can make an exception in your case. It's not good for you to sit moping all by yourself. You must make an effort to cheer up, look on the sunny side of things.'

'Sister's always like that,' said Eileen. 'That's why nobody ever asks her anything.' She sympathized much more with Irene now she was in opposition to Sister; before that she had said to Linda, 'I can't think what she's got against OT,' but now she said, 'I can't think why they have to make her do it if she don't want to. It's not like physio – it's not doing her any good.' To Irene she said, 'Once they've got you in here they think they can push you around. I guess that's what Mr Pollard couldn't stand.'

At the mention of Mr Pollard Irene pricked up her ears and asked Eileen what she knew about him.

'He's some sort of an inventor,' said Eileen. 'Everyone's talking about him, but I don't really know much. He weren't in here long. He discharged himself, more or less, but he still comes for treatment. Miss Howell is mad about him.'

'She didn't seem very pleased about this harness he'd made.'

'She don't want nobody interfering in her department, that's why.'

'It was a jolly good harness.'

'That don't make no difference. They're all the same – they want to be little tin gods in their own department.'

Irene drank in all the gossip Eileen could tell her about the hospital, glad that it reflected badly on people she found difficult. She had come to rely on Eileen for company; she felt very isolated in the ward and she missed her mother more than she had expected. Eileen was always ready to linger and chat, neglecting her other duties. She was constantly in trouble with Sister which was hardly surprising, as she was untidy and happy-go-lucky and had a knack of forgetting things. Even Linda criticized Eileen : 'I can't think what made her take up nursing,' she said to Irene. 'She says she's accident prone, but I'd call it just plain clumsy.'

Irene would hear nothing against Eileen. 'She has a loving heart. She wants to help people. I suppose that's why she became a nurse,' she said.

Linda was kind too, but much more brisk and efficient. She had not made a special favourite of Irene, and did not tell her all her own affairs, as Eileen did. Irene had at first a very confused idea of Eileen's love life and the various boys she went about with. The names of Les and Terry cropped up frequently and it was some time before she grasped that Les was Linda's boyfriend and Terry was his friend whom Eileen worshipped from afar. Eileen was tall and gangly and her face was one mass of pimples. She was always trying some new method of getting rid of them. She went without chocolate for five whole days and then could stand it no longer and ate three Mars bars without stopping. She was always making a fool of herself in her unashamed pursuit of Terry, and Irene in all seriousness advised her to play hard-to-get. 'Couldn't you pretend you were going out with one of the doctors?' she suggested. She had always heard that nurses fall for doctors.

'Not a hope!' exclaimed Eileen. 'Terry knows already what doctors we have here. Nasrullah has a wife and kids back at home, and the Turk don't speak no English. I mean, I don't have anything against him 'cos he's not English – I'm not like that – but it do make conversation a bit difficult. And then there's Dr Neale – well, I ask you!'

Irene did not know why Dr Neale was so far out of the question. It made her realize all of a sudden how much in the dark she was in these matters, she who had never been out with a boy; and she felt a pang of envy. Not that she envied Eileen her particular life – she did not want to be in foolish pursuit of a youth who had blue eyes like Paul Newman (the only distinguishing fact about Terry that Eileen had been able to give her) – but she felt herself cut off from the normal life of other girls of her age, like the Lady of Shalott in her island castle.

Her uncle had brought her the poem. 'I only had it in weighty anthologies or collected works,' he said, 'but I went round to your place and luckily caught sight of this on the shelf. It's your own.' He opened the flyleaf to show her 'Irene Paxton Upper III' written in a round childish hand. It was the same dingy green school book she remembered, which brought back with it all the odour of school corridors and dormitories and ink-stained desks. When he had gone she read the poem over and over again. It was different from what she remembered; she had forgotten all the pseudo-archaic colour and her first impression was disappointing – it was all pastiche. I can see why Uncle William was so superior about it, she thought. Lines such as

A bow-shot from her bower eaves

brought to mind the sepia reproductions from Watts and the Pre-Raphaelites which hung in those same corridors at school. They failed to evoke anything more remote than Victorian make-believe.

Yet something was left in her mind after all, a mood, a mythical truth which went beyond Victoriana and indeed beyond any actual age or period, which made her read the poem over again. She loved the description of the view from the window:

There she sees the highway near
Winding down to Camelot:
There the river eddy whirls,
And there the surly village-churls,
And the red cloaks of market girls,
Pass onward from Shalott.

Sometimes a troop of damsels glad,
An abbot on an ambling pad,
Sometimes a curly shepherd-lad,
Goes by to towered Camelot;
And sometimes thro' the mirror blue
The knights come riding two and two:
She hath no loyal knight and true,
The Lady of Shalott.

But in her web she still delights
To weave the mirror's magic sights,
For often thro' the silent nights
A funeral, with plumes and lights,
And music, went to Camelot,
Or when the moon was overhead,
Came two young lovers lately wed,
'I am half sick of shadows,' said
The Lady of Shalott.

Her uncle had spoken of a fresco in Siena which this brought to mind, but she was glad that he had failed to find the reproduction because for her it was the view from the hospital window and the people who went to and fro along the lane. She identified so closely with the content of the poem that she could not read certain lines without a lump in her throat and a prick of tears in her eyes – such lines as

Seeing all his own mischance –

Life would pass her by; it was her fate never to love, never to mix, to be cut off by her illness from all the joys, simple and profound, to which other girls like Linda and Eileen, or Clare and Diana, could look forward. In the end she put away the book and resolved never to read it again, because it encouraged her to wallow in self-pity. Yet the poem remained in her mind.

Unfortunately business had taken her uncle off on a trip to Turkey and the only visitor she could still expect was her father. She looked forward to that. At home he would sometimes come into her room and say, 'Do you want to get out of the house?' He was perhaps only going down to the end of the farm, but he guessed how trapped she felt, how the smallest change of scene would be a relief, even if it only meant sitting in the car and staring at a haystack while he was busy. She always enjoyed being with him; they never talked much, but they understood one another.

But when he came to the hospital he was a fish out of water. It seemed necessary to talk about something. He got up; he sat down; he went over to the window. For him the view from the window was a crop of beet which was doing badly because of the dry weather. Before he left he confided to Irene that his blood pressure was high.

'It's nothing much,' he hastened to add. 'You mustn't mention a word of it to your mother.'

'You're doing too much,' said Irene. 'Try and get some rest.'

'It isn't easy at this time of year,' he said.

'You mustn't dream of driving all the way over here when you're tired.'

She saw the look of relief pass over his face although he protested, 'I promised your mother.'

'I won't let on,' she said.

Afterwards she cried. She had been banking on his visits. She had even hoped that, with her mother away, they would talk about things they never did talk about at home. But instead, even their customary tacit understanding seemed to have been lost, a casualty to the institutional atmosphere. Her tears did not go long unnoticed.

'No need to be so miserable – the world's not coming to an

47

end,' said Mrs Boundy in her usual loud voice. 'When you've reached my age you'll know what it is to cry.' She proceeded to tell a story which she had told many times before, of how Mr Boundy had gone into hospital for a minor operation and died unexpectedly under the anaesthetic. This was to her the ultimate in tragedy and gave her more right to cry than anyone else. As soon as Mrs Boundy had left the ward on a call of nature there was a general outcry.

'Don't you take no notice of her.'

'Must've been a blessed relief for her old man.'

'Was it bad news?' they asked.

Irene stifled her tears. 'No, it's nothing,' she said. 'I'm just being silly.' It was always like that – they longed to sympathize but there was never anything to tell them, so they thought she was stand-offish. Only Birdie would understand and Irene was relieved when she came over to talk to her, bringing with her the artefact she was making in occupational therapy.

'You're so clever,' said Birdie, 'you can tell me what I've done wrong.' She held it up for Irene to see. 'Your dad don't look too well,' she said.

Irene told her about the blood pressure. 'I told him he mustn't come again. We don't seem to have anything to say to one another, anyway. Oh Birdie, why is it I can't talk to him? I was so looking forward to his visit.'

'I've seen it time and again,' said Birdie, 'but I don't know the reason. It's the same with children. I often think it's a good thing my Nellie lives too far away to come visiting. I want to see her but when she comes I end up watching the clock, waiting for her to leave. I must be an unnatural mother, I think – but then I reckon it's because they worry too much about us. Your mum talks a lot and your dad he says nothing, but you can easy see they both worry themselves silly over you. And worrying don't do nobody no good, but they can't help it. It's just the way it is.'

'It happens to other people?' said Irene.

'Course it do, love. You don't want to go thinking your dad don't want to see you, no more than you don't want to see him.

48

But what's the good of seeing folks when we just upset ourselves about it? You've done the best thing you could, sending him and your mum away.'

Meanwhile Irene had been examining Birdie's artefact. 'It's there. Look, you've missed out a nail,' she said.

'So I have. You mean I've got to undo it right back to there?'

'If you want to get it perfect. What are you going to do with it when it's finished, Birdie?'

Birdie guessed Irene's thought so she said mockingly, 'I daresay they can cut the string off it and give it to someone else to do again.'

'That's all they're good for,' said Irene bitterly.

'I'm sure she'd let you do something different,' said Birdie. 'Why don't you talk to her?'

'I don't want to do the other things either.' The occupational therapist had already suggested all sorts of alternatives. 'I'd rather just read, but it's difficult to do that in a room that's full of people talking.'

'Miss Benstead don't like OT no more than you do,' said Birdie. 'D'you remember Miss Benstead? I got a letter this morning and she's coming in to join us this week.'

Irene dimly remembered Miss Benstead – Bedstead as the nurses called her, but never to her face because Miss Benstead didn't stand for that sort of thing. 'She's been a school teacher,' explained Birdie. 'She don't take kindly to being treated like she was a little kid. You know how some nurses are. She won't let them order her around like they do us. She always has to know the reason.'

'We all ought to be like that,' said Irene. 'Then this place would have to change.'

'I dunno. It's like this – if a nurse gets in the mood to order you around, better ask no questions, because she'll only take it out on someone else if you do.'

'You're too good, Birdie,' said Irene. 'I wish I were like you.'

Birdie laughed. 'You stay being yourself. It takes all sorts,' she said.

49

But what Birdie said did make Irene wonder: was she fighting for fair treatment at the expense of other people? That evening something happened to make her ashamed of her resentment against Sister about the bed. The other patients were going off to the dayroom for their supper when old Mrs Rawson stopped at the foot of her bed. They had never spoken before and at first Irene could not catch what she said.

'You're a dwarf, like me, dearie,' she repeated. 'That's what my husband always says to me: You're a dwarf, Edith. Sister says she ain't never had so many dwarfs all in at one time. Never mind though, there'll be other folks going out at the end of the week, I daresay. I'm sure I don't know why they has to make the beds so high, but I reckon it's men. They're all the same – they'd never think of some folks not having legs as long as them. My old man, he's six foot two. He's a policeman.' It appeared that PC Rawson was always doing things about the house, but whenever he put up a shelf it was way out of his wife's reach and she had to stand on a chair to get things off it. 'And I can't go clambering about on chairs at my time of life, can I?' she said. 'Dr Roberts says to me, "I don't know what Mr Harris is going to say, when I tells him you've been climbing about on top of the furniture again." That's what he says.'

Mrs Rawson had suddenly become human and Irene blushed to think that she had been so arrogant as to imagine that she, Irene, had a better right to the low bed. Perhaps Sister had acted fairly after all. Irene remembered her earlier resolve to accept the hospital and all the people in it, even the difficult ones, and she decided to make a new start. She would make friends with Mrs Rawson, by way of making up for all the unkind rebellious thoughts she had had about her. She would stop fighting, accept what life offered and see good in all the people around her.

Chapter VII

I t was hard for Irene to see any good in occupational therapy, but she tried to resign herself to it as a necessary evil. Perhaps she could make friends with Miss Benstead when she came in and together they could besiege Sister. Meanwhile she said no to Eileen's repeated offers to help her play truant.

The OT room was at the other end of the building and to get there they had to go along miles of corridors punctuated at intervals by heavy swing doors. These doors were a fire precaution to prevent a blaze spreading rapidly through the hospital, but they were a serious hazard to anyone who had not the strength of ten. No one who walked with sticks or crutches or whose balance was precarious could hope to get through without assistance; no one could wheel a chair through unless someone able bodied held the door open.

'It must have been men thought up these fire doors,' said Irene to Mrs Rawson.

'Yes, dear, it is hot today,' that lady, who was very deaf, replied.

'The DOORS,' said Irene pointing towards them. 'Only MEN could have designed such stupid DOORS.'

'What, dear?' Mrs Rawson followed her gesture with a puzzled look. Then she brightened and nodded. 'Yes, I was watching that on telly last night.'

Irene gave up the attempt to communicate, and smiled and nodded too.

As they went down the corridor one nurse would abandon her wheelchair and go ahead to hold the door open. When the rest of the procession had gone through she would come back for her patient and someone else would hold the door back for them. Eileen was pushing Irene. She went forward to hold the last door open. The rest of the procession went through. Eileen let the door swing to and went on with the others.

It was typical of Eileen – no wonder she got on Sister's nerves. In a moment she would realize and come back. Irene was preparing to laugh at her. But instead she heard the clatter of footsteps as the nurses went up the main stairs to their common room. She had been forgotten.

The corridor was a long avenue of brown lino with a brown gloss dado to shoulder height. There were geriatric wards on either side and the only daylight came in through glass panels over the doors. There was no one about. It seemed an age before Irene heard a door open somewhere behind her. She could not turn round to look as there was too little play in her joints, but she raised her voice and called out, 'Excuse me.'

She could hear someone moving behind her, shuffling, dragging steps on the lino. He was muttering to himself under his breath, whoever he was. He came level with her and she could see him in his dressing-gown with the cord trailing, his slippers half covered by the pyjama legs which were too long. He was dribbling. He seemed unaware of her presence. The door behind them opened and swung to once more. Sharp peremptory footsteps sounded on the lino.

'Where do you think you're off to this time, Grandad?' demanded the nurse. She took him by the arm and swung him so that he looked Irene in the face, but his eye was vacant and he did not see her. He made no protest, offered no resistance, but allowed himself to be led back the way he had come. Irene remembered, too late, to raise her voice.

'Please do you think you could just . . .'

The door closed. Nothing happened. She had the impression that the nurse had not seen her either.

Irene began to cry. How stupid! she told herself angrily – you don't even want to go to OT. Yet the tears streamed down her face. There was something terrible about old age when it had lost all dignity – that mindless drooling old man led off by the bright bossy nurse. The bleak institutional corridor with its brown lino seemed a place without hope, an underworld in which they confined the bleating, aimless shadows of what had once been people.

Then the fire doors ahead of her opened. Mavis stood staring at her in amazement.

'Whatever be you a-doing of here?' she asked.

'They left me behind,' said Irene, her voice coming out between sobs.

'There, there, don't cry, love. Mavis'll look after you. Where was you a-going when they left you here?'

'OT,' said Irene.

Mavis took hold of the chair and then paused as if a thought had struck her. 'Look, love, d'you want to go to OT?' she asked.

'Not really, but I suppose I'd better. Sister won't let us stay in the ward.'

Mavis leant on the back of the chair for a moment. Then she swung it round and set off back down the corridor.

'Where are you taking me, Mavis?' asked Irene.

'It's me afternoon off. I thought maybe you'd like to come and see my place just for a change.'

Irene scarcely dared to believe her ears. 'The little wood that isn't a wood?' she asked uncertainly.

'You'll see when we get there. Like I told you, it ain't a wood at all.'

They reversed through the fire doors, which swung back scraping the side of the chair. Opposite the lift was a passage leading to the back of the hospital. They came out amongst bicycle sheds and dustbins and set off towards the right.

'We have to go round,' said Mavis. 'But it's not far. Mr Pollard comes over every day by hisself, to go in the pool.'

'Walking?' asked Irene.

'In a chair,' said Mavis. 'He has the use of his arms, you see. I don't rightly know how he come to this hospital, 'cos he don't have the arthritis. He smashed himself up in his motor.'

'Is that why he doesn't live in?' said Irene.

'Oh no. He was in the hospital to begin with. But he couldn't take it. The thing about Mr Pollard is, he ain't used to being ill, not like most folks in Granstead is. I guess he's mostly used to getting his own way. Miss Howell, she hates having outpatients, but Mr Harris, he agreed, so she has to put up with it.'

They had been going down the back drive and now they turned off into an estate of bijou modern residences with fancy names done in pokerwork on obtuse slices of rustic wood. Irene was just about to cry out with educated derision at the sight of a child-sized wishing well built of real bricks, when Mavis proudly informed her, 'Me nephew Neil lives there. You never seen anything so posh.'

They turned again, down a road that presently became a track. The long bleak red brick posterior of the hospital came into view.

'So that's what it's like,' said Irene. She had never seen the hospital from the back, as she had always approached it by its ornate main front. Astronauts looking back at the world when it has become a mere ball in the sky may know something of what she felt, looking back across the fields at the place which was her whole world for the time being.

Mavis paused. 'I'm puffed,' she said. 'Mind if I take a little rest? These chairs weren't built for nothing but indoors.'

'Don't take me any further,' said Irene. 'The road's too rough – you'll hurt yourself. You don't know what it means to me to've come this far and seen the hospital looking small and unimportant.'

But Mavis had other ideas. 'I'm showing you your wood, don't you remember?' she said, setting off again.

Irene protested. For the first time she began to fear the consequences of this outing. Supposing by now they were searching the hospital for her?

'Please, Mavis – '

'Are you all right, love?'

'*I'm* all right – '

'I don't want to jolt you too much.'

'I'm thinking of you, Mavis.'

'Wait till you see this new wheelchair Mr Pollard's a-making

54

of – it'll do anything, 'cept fly. Now just tell me if you can see that blessed wood of yours yet.'

Strange to say, Mavis was quite right: there was no wood. It was all a trick of perspective. There were trees, certainly, but they were spaced out along the hedgerows, one here, one there. From the hospital they had appeared as a group. The lane twisted round and skirted a garden, of which she could scarcely catch a glimpse because of the dense screen of trees and shrubs along its margin. They came through a gate, which stood open, into a farmyard. Mavis paused and took breath.

The first thing that struck Irene about the place was the peace. She could hear a bird moving in the treetops. The afternoon sun slanted down through the leaves. A ginger and white cat crossing the yard saw her and paused, one paw still lifted; then decided she was of no account and went on upon its own business.

The quiet of the place grew upon her. Only then did she begin to notice signs that it was unoccupied. The sun fell full on the comfortable old house half covered in honeysuckle and roses. But the rambling rose was falling away from the house in an entanglement that blocked the path to the door, and the honeysuckle had climbed up over the roof and insinuated itself inside the window frames. She saw that the windows were shuttered.

'Does nobody live here?' she asked.

'He lives at the back, does Mr Pollard,' said Mavis in explanation.

The house lay in a hollow. The farmyard sloped down towards it; apart from the track the yard was overgrown with nettles and elder, in the midst of which Irene could catch a glimpse of derelict farm machinery and of some abandoned plastic toy which had lost its colour in an unhealthy way, like an ice lolly when you suck the synthetic juice from it. There was a pond beyond this undergrowth, dark water at the foot of the garden wall, overhung by a sprawling buddleia. A swarm of gnats hung in the air above the surface of the water and there were butterflies, a russet orange, on the mauve spires of the buddleia flowers. Irene was struck by the silence of the butter-flies as she never had been before : they rose and fluttered and resettled and not the smallest rustle of sound did they make.

'It is a very peaceful place,' she said, 'But why has it been left so deserted?'

'Nobody's lived here since years back, till Mr Pollard come,' said Mavis.

Irene gave up asking questions. Mavis started to wheel her across the farmyard to the back of the house. There was a range of barns up the side of the hill, their tiled roofs sagging and cushioned with moss. Behind the house was a long low build-ing, not nearly so picturesque. Mavis made for this. The wide doors stood open allowing the sun to enter. They went in.

The floor was of concrete, sloping towards a drain which ran down the centre. At one side a massive work bench had been recently built. It took Irene a moment to accustom her eyes to the interior. Then she saw Mr Pollard. He had his back to them and was working at a drawing board. He had heard them enter and as soon as he had finished what he was doing he pushed aside the board, released the brake on his chair and allowed it to roll backwards down the slope. It ran fast, in a curve, went a little way up the opposite slope and then came to rest across the gutter facing them. The very speed with which he allowed the chair to move marked him as an outsider; Irene knew he would never have done that if he had suffered from arthritis, for fear of a jolt.

'You came all the way here in that?' he said in surprise. 'They're not meant for cross-country treks.' He seemed more surprised at her means of transport than at her sudden appear-ance, almost as if he had been expecting her. In fact the next thing he said was, 'You're Ireen? Or do you call it Irene?'

'It doesn't really matter,' said Irene, supposing Mavis must have given him her version of the name. 'But my mother minds – she likes me to be called Irene.'

'Names like that are a nuisance,' he said. 'My first wife was called Eunice. Some people used to call her You-nicey. One can't always be correcting people and yet they feel embarrassed

56

when they find out they've been saying it wrong – or else they get aggressive and insist theirs is the only correct pronunciation. And this is my friend Harriet,' he added.

All Irene could see of Harriet was a shadow cast on the sunlit floor, whose appearance she had noticed a moment before. She turned as far as she was able, but Harriet did not come forward when she was introduced, nor give her any greeting.

Meanwhile Mr Pollard had gone on talking about wheel-chairs. 'It seems to me the suspension could be enormously improved and that would bring with it a number of benefits, particularly in cases like yours. But of course nobody's going to spend money on a project like that. The government is happy to waste millions on Concorde, but as we all know they won't spend an extra half penny piece on the invalid car. I used to work in the aircraft industry before my accident so I know the endless money and ingenuity that goes to make a few people shoot around the world even faster than before, furthering the cause of big business.'

It was the sort of thing Irene might have said herself – sometimes had – but for some reason of which she was scarcely even aware, he annoyed her. She thought she found him arrogant. 'There is someone who does a lot of work on wheel-chairs,' she said drily. 'A girl I met last summer has an electric chair he made. He says so long as you can move one finger he can give you a chair you can operate yourself. But if you've got arthritis you've got to keep moving. It's a mistake to live in a chair.'

'I know who you mean,' he said. 'I've met him. We're going to pool ideas. He's done nothing about suspension so far. I know wheelchairs have to be designed individually – you may only want a wheelchair for cross-country treks, while someone else needs one to get from the stove to the sink.'

Irene bit her lip – he obviously knew a bit more about things than she supposed. But he did not seem to have taken offence at her tone of rebuke. 'You see, suspension is my hobby horse,' he went on, ' – I even have a well-sprung hobby horse. I was working on a type of sprung wheel for aeroplanes. The nearer you get your suspension to the source of friction – i.e. to the surface over which your vehicle is to run – the better. You can intercept the bumps before they reach the frame. Harriet – can you get out Granny's wonderful chair?'

'Granny's wonderful chair?' asked Irene.

'Harriet calls it that. She has an unscientific mind and it reminds her of a book she had as a child about a magic chair which went wherever you asked it to, even upstairs.'

'Oh, I don't believe that,' said Irene. 'Even magic must have its limitations.'

That made him smile. 'Can I explain to you about these wheels, or will it bore you?' Harriet had come in with a most strange wheelchair. The seat part of it was an old upholstered chair with wooden arms; the wheels were fairly wide, like miniature stream-roller wheels and instead of spokes there were flexible plates so that the hub sprung about, not always remaining in the centre of the circle. But it was more complicated than that; he began to tell her about castor action and piston action, things she did not understand at all, and her attention wandered from the chair to Harriet, who for the first time had come into her field of vision. She observed her covertly: a slight boyish figure with brown hair, tied back but with little curly wisps escaping at the temples, brown eyes with long lashes and a creamy complexion. She saw that Harriet was beautiful; she also saw that Harriet avoided looking at her, at her crippled body and her moon-like face, bloated by taking steroid drugs.

'I would like you to try it,' Mr Pollard was saying. 'You would be doing me a favour, as your comments would be valuable to me. Also it would afford you a more comfortable journey back to the hospital.'

Chapter VIII

W H E N she had sat down in the wonderful chair Mr Pollard proposed that Harriet should take her for a tour of the premises. 'The roughest roads possible, and you'll see how the wheels cope.' Irene found she had sailed out of the building without even feeling the threshold.

'Can I see where you live, Mavis?' she called. Mavis had remained inside.

'Course you can, love,' said Mavis. 'Miss Harriet'll take you.'

Harriet set off without a word. Irene found the silent presence behind her something of a challenge and she was determined to provoke a response. 'I feel as if I were dreaming and if I don't see everything before I wake up, I never shall. You are all dream people to me, only half real,' – let her prove she's real, she thought – 'Or rather, I think of you as people in a picture, because I have only seen you all as a view from the hospital window.'

All Harriet said was, 'Glebe Cottage isn't much to look at, but we can go there if you like.'

'I don't mind what it looks like. I have to see it to believe in it. In a picture you can never see what lies round the corner. I have lain long hours looking at this place. I thought I knew every leaf on every tree, but now I've got here it turns out to be a different place. I don't know quite what I expected. Perhaps I thought that there'd be nothing behind the trees except the canvas they were painted on.'

After a pause Harriet said, not very graciously, 'I suppose the hospital is just a picture to me. At least, we've always called it a blot on the landscape, and that must be a metaphor from painting.'

Irene felt as if she had received a slap in the face. It was probably not meant as such, but that made it all the more galling. These people thought of the hospital – her life and all those other lives inside it – as no more than a blot, an ugly blemish they tried to ignore. 'I know it's ugly,' she said and they went on in silence.

They had turned up past the long barns. The track went uphill and began to peter out. For Irene the whole afternoon had gone sour. She could remember that first breathtaking entry into the world beyond the window: the sight of the hospital from afar; how the wood had dissolved before her eyes; coming into the farmyard and how the peace of the place descended on her, and that ginger and white cat pausing, its paw lifted, watching them. But something had gone wrong since. Why had she felt so hostile to Mr Pollard? Why was Harriet so unfriendly? And what were they doing all this time at the hospital? With growing nervousness Irene pictured a panic-stricken Eileen . . . How long would it be before they had to tell Sister? Meanwhile the wonderful chair was forging uphill, laying waste as it went. Irene was amazed at the way it breasted all obstacles. No vehicle had come along here for many a long season and the balk between the two wheel tracks had grown high with plants. Ahead of her it was a lovely sight, behind her a mash of leaves. The desire to see Mavis's cottage had died within her.

'Don't let's go any further,' she said. 'I ought to go back, you know. They'll be wondering what's become of me at the hospital.' Harriet had come willingly to a stop and Irene asked her, 'What are those great plants with the big white velvety leaves? It seems a pity to bruise them so.'

'Mullein,' replied Harriet. She picked up a leaf that had broken off and laid it in Irene's lap. It was the first spontaneous gesture she had made and Irene was touched. She stroked the soft nap on the leaf. 'Country is so tender,' she said, recalling a poem. 'I felt, when I first arrived here, a peace about the place as if it was far, far away from the madding crowd, from the world of Granstead or from that estate of bijou residences we passed through on the way here. It was a sort of lost domain, forgotten here among the trees.' Irene sat there stroking the mullein leaf, trying to recall that something she had lost. She paid no attention to Harriet, musing more for her own benefit than for the sake of communication. But something had lit up suddenly in Harriet.

'Those bijou residences didn't exist when I was a child,' she said. 'This was a dairy farm then and the cows grazed on the meadows opposite where I live, where the estate is now.'

'Why is this place deserted?' asked Irene. 'I feel it is a kindly place and yet it has the air of being long abandoned.'

It was a tale that Harriet was pleased to narrate, but she told it in her own order. 'When I was a little girl, Mr Busby lived in Glebe Farm – he was the farmer. Where Mr Pollard has his workshop was the milking parlour, and the place where he keeps the wonderful chair was the coldstore. In those days Mavis was the milkmaid and if we wanted cream or forgot to ask for more milk we came round here to fetch it. I used to love to come to the Glebe in those days. Mavis was my favourite person and this was my favourite place.

'Then one time Mr Busby was kicked by a cow. It was during a difficult calving. That year the cows were all served by a special prize bull, and they were got with calves too big for them to carry and they mostly had to be aborted. It was a year of disasters. Mr Busby's back was so badly injured that he had to give up the farm and they went to live in a bungalow by the seaside. Those meadows were sold for development and another farmer took over the rest of the farm. He already lived somewhere else, so he never came to live in the house.

'About that time they built the pool over at the hospital – I daresay you know all about that – and Mavis went to work there. Her brother still worked for the farmer, so they still lived at Glebe Cottage.'

'And nobody has lived at the farm since then? How long ago was that?' asked Irene.

'I must have been five. My brother was about two, because he adored the builders and all their diggers and bulldozers. He used to stand at the gate crowing for joy, all day long. And I hated it.'

'And now you are?'

'Seventeen, so that makes it twelve years ago.'

'What happened to the farmhouse?'

'At one time the farmer put one of his labourers in here. The man had a huge family so he thought the big house would suit them, but they hated the place. They said it was haunted. It was never haunted before they came!' said Harriet contemptuously. 'The people who lived in the new houses made up stories about the place, that was all. There was a huge wardrobe Mr Busby had left behind because it wouldn't go into the new bungalow and they put it across the door of one of the bedrooms, to keep the ghosts from coming out. It's still there.

'They made a wilderness of the place. They left an old mattress in the garden, and some car tyres and loads of old rubbish. After that the house stood empty until Mr Pollard came. I used to come here a lot to be by myself. It is a sort of lost place like you said.' While she had been talking she had come to sit on the grass in front of Irene. She smiled up at her.

'So it's still your favourite place. Perhaps you don't like strangers who come barging in?'

'Of course you can come – you're welcome,' Harriet said hastily. She spoke hastily because she did resent intruders – that was true. She had not been too pleased to show Irene round. 'It doesn't *belong* to me.'

'There are all sorts of belonging,' said Irene, 'apart from owning a place. You know, I even half thought it belonged to me, because it was *my* view from the window and nobody else bothered to look at it.'

At that moment Mavis appeared at the bottom of the track. 'Ain't you got no further than that?' she called in surprise. 'He's all ready to take them photos now.'

Harriet jumped up with alacrity.

'Photos?' asked Irene in surprise.

'Purely for scientific purposes,' said Harriet. She seemed

pleased for no reason. 'He takes film and then plays it back in slow motion so that he can see how the wheels really react.'

Irene had forgotten about the hospital whilst she and Harriet were talking, but as soon as the filming was over she began to fret again. Mr Pollard assured her that her fears were exaggerated.

'They won't bother,' he said. 'The most they'll have done is send someone to see if you're still sitting in the corridor. When they find you're not there they'll assume someone else is looking after you.'

'Yes, but time's getting on and they'll start to worry as soon as they get back to the ward. Apart from anything else, they put me to bed then.' She had to explain about the high bed.

'That place is so disorganized it's past belief!' exclaimed Mr Pollard. 'There must be lower beds.'

'You're wrong – there aren't any lower beds. It just happens that they've got an abnormal number of dwarfs in at the same time.' She felt annoyed with Mr Pollard. What right had he to criticize the hospital? She was ashamed now of her own earlier resentment and felt a surge of loyalty when he attacked the hospital.

'What do you do with yourself all evening?' he asked. 'Do you read much?'

'It's difficult for me to read in bed,' she said, 'but I read poetry because it comes in slim volumes that do not tire my hands and, besides, you can read a little at a time and ponder over it.'

'What about a bookrest?' said Mr Pollard. 'I'm not an inventor for nothing. I made one for myself once, purely for comfort, so that I could read in bed without getting my hands cold. I'll do a drawing and see if Neil can have it made for me – Mavis's nephew, you know? He produced those wheels for me at the engineering works where he's employed.'

Mavis beamed proudly. Irene was amazed at this generous offer. She felt she had been anything but gracious to Mr Pollard. 'It's very kind of you to suggest it,' she said.

'Next time you come,' said Mr Pollard, 'I want to show you some film.'

The words brought Irene up with a jolt. 'But I can't come again,' she said.

'You must!' he said in a manner of jovial threat. 'I don't believe in can't. Mavis said she couldn't bring you at all and the very next day she brings you. I want you to see my film of patients in the pool. I need your advice in modifying the harness. You're the only person who has made a constructive suggestion so far.'

Would he ever believe what a chain of utter coincidence had brought her to the Glebe that afternoon? Irene felt irritated with him again, because he could not see how her life was circumscribed. Not wishing to show her irritation, she asked, 'You've taken film of patients in the pool?'

'Of the men. The silly old bird won't even let me watch the women at play. I don't know what indecency she thinks I'm likely to commit.'

Suddenly Irene could contain her irritation no longer. 'I think it's jolly open-minded of her to let you take film of the men,' she exclaimed. 'It's not the sort of thing most patients expect to do, after all.'

'It's not a prison, you know,' said Mr Pollard. 'A hospital should be open to change. Don't go getting patient mentality.'

'I often wish I were more patient,' said Irene tartly.

After a pause Mr Pollard said, 'You're right, of course. It is open-minded of Miss Howell to let a cynical old rogue like me, quite without status in the hospital, do experiments in her pool. But you'll come, won't you?'

'How can I?' said Irene, penitent but still exasperated.

He looked at Mavis. 'Can't she?'

Mavis looked uncomfortable. 'Like I told you before, Mr Pollard, patients ain't supposed to leave the hospital grounds 'cos of insurance.'

'We've been through all this before. Jock Brett slips out regularly to buy himself fish and chips, and he's not the only one. In the men's wards they know the rules are only there to be broken.'

'Poor Mavis!' Irene exclaimed indignantly. 'Don't you understand? She works there. She can't afford to lose her job.'

'I could come and fetch you,' said Harriet suddenly.

She could so easily have said, 'I could go and fetch her.' Irene was so used to being spoken of in the third person like a piece of baggage that she was almost surprised that the offer was addressed to her personally. But before she could reply, Mr Pollard had spoken for her.

'Splendid,' he said. 'Go back with them now, Harriet, and you can measure up the bedhead. I shall have to work out a means of attaching the bookrest. I'll tell you what measurements I need.'

Chapter IX

BIRDIE noticed that Irene was missing but she had heard about Eileen's plan to leave her by the vending machine in the hallway so when somebody else asked what had become of 'the little girl' she tipped them the wink to keep quiet. Mrs Boundy saw this interchange and bellowed out, 'Playing truant again, is she? Got her boyfriend visiting?' She explained to the occupational therapist, as if it were established fact, that Irene had a visitor and Sister had let them stay up in the ward.

So it was not until the nurses came to fetch the patients away that the truth came out.

'What's become of Ireen?' Eileen said, looking round.

Birdie was surprised. 'I thought you were plotting something with her,' she said.

'Oh no,' said Eileen, 'we decided against that.'

'Well, where did you take her?'

'I brought her in here, didn't I?'

'I've not seen Ireen this afternoon,' said the occupational therapist. 'I was told she had a visitor.'

'But she came down in the lift with us,' said Birdie.

'Of course she came down in the lift,' exclaimed Eileen. 'I was pushing her, weren't I?'

'You know what,' said Linda ' – you left her behind in the corridor. Now I come to think of it, she wasn't with us when we crossed the hall.'

Appalled, Eileen dashed off to look in the corridor, and in the corner by the vending machine where they had once planned to stow Irene.

'Somebody must have taken her back to the ward,' said Linda. 'You are a fool, Eileen. Let this be a lesson to you.'

All the way back to the ward Eileen kept on saying, 'I don't know how I did it! You'd think somebody would have told me.' She was very relieved to find Irene safe and sound in the ward and rushed up to her exclaiming, 'I don't know how I did it! Can you ever forgive me? Poor Ireen! Whatever became of you? How could I forget you, of all people! I ought to have my head seen to.'

'She must have left her brains at home when she came this morning,' said Linda. In the end everyone was laughing and it became a joke that Eileen was the world's worst scatterbrain.

Irene was relieved that no one had missed her during the afternoon, but she felt a little hurt all the same. She did not feel at all inclined to tell Eileen her adventures. 'Mavis brought me back to the ward,' she said – a statement which was strictly true. 'People must pass up and down that corridor all the time – there was no need for you to worry, except that it might have been Sister who passed by. So thank your stars it was only Mavis.'

Eileen gasped at the thought that it might have been Sister. 'But I deserved it,' she added ruefully. 'It ought really to have been Sister.'

'Well, I'm glad it was Mavis,' said Irene. Eileen sounded so penitent that later, while she was being put to bed, Irene relented and told her, 'It turned out very well for me. As it was such a fine afternoon Mavis took me out for a little walk.'

'That was nice,' said Eileen. 'The gardens are real nice at the moment. We could take you down into the garden sometime if you wanted, you know.'

'I'm too much trouble to you already,' said Irene.

'You're no trouble at all! We'll take you down into the garden one day. You can sit and read there. You'd like that, wouldn't you? And I won't forget to bring you in, either!' Eileen was eager to do something to make up for having forgotten her.

'It would be nice,' said Irene. It was a very kind suggestion and she was surprised that Eileen understood that she would want to sit out there alone and read. She smiled up at her so gratefully that Eileen suddenly put her arms round her and kissed her.

'You do forgive me, don't you?' she said.

Afterwards, lying in bed, she was glad she had not told Eileen anything more about her outing. She felt confused by the afternoon. Her feelings were very mixed, but uppermost came a wish that it had never happened at all. There had been some good moments. When Harriet had sat down on the over-grown track and told her the story of the place she had suddenly thought, We could be friends; again, when Harriet said, 'I could come and fetch you,' she thought that Harriet must have the same idea. But all this was swallowed up in her annoyance with Mr Pollard. How dare he be so high-handed with her and with Mavis? She found herself mentally arguing with him in defence of the hospital. She was almost angry with him about the bookrest because she would have to feel grateful; she de-cided the offer would come to nothing and then felt angry with him for having raised her hopes only to disappoint them.

They had been in a great hurry on the return journey as Irene was anxious to get back to the ward before the party returned from OT. It was only when Harriet was measuring the bedhead that she found time to tell her that she really couldn't go out of the hospital grounds. 'It's all very well for Mr Pollard,' she said. 'He'll never have to come back here again. But the rest of us who suffer from arthritis are going to come in and out of this hospital for the rest of our lives so we have to keep the peace. I don't know what happens in the men's wards but up here we abide by the rules and I'm going to stay that way.' She had seen the sulky look on Harriet's face and added, 'Please try to understand: it's not because I don't want to come.'

Gazing out of the window from her bed she had tried to compose the trees into a little wood, but obstinately they re-asserted themselves as single trees scattered along a hedgerow. She could not see the house, but she could distinguish the screen of trees that ran long the edge of the garden and hid it from view. Knowing it and having gone there, she could never see it again as she had seen it day by day during the past weeks. It was like lost innocence, never to be regained. She was glad she had not told Eileen; she did not want to talk about it with anyone; she half hoped she would forget she had been there.

Next day when she went down to the pool, Mavis said to her, 'Miss Harriet took a great liking to you.' She did not know whether to be pleased or not, and see-sawed from one extreme to the other. She had hoped Harriet and she might be friends, and she did need friends; but on the other hand she was afraid of disappointment. Also she would prefer to keep out of Mr Pollard's way as he only irritated her and she did not want to have to fight to keep the hospital rules. Perhaps Harriet would come and visit her and take her down into the garden, an idea which had begun to appeal to her since Eileen had suggested it. That seemed such a delightful prospect that she immediately had to defend herself against the probability that it would be disappointed. It was safer to rely on Eileen than to build wild hopes on Harriet. Eileen had a heart of gold, while Harriet was an unknown quantity.

It was a Thursday, the day the big men, the consultants and surgeons, came down from London to see their patients and perform operations, so no visitors were allowed. Irene was relieved that she need neither hope for nor dread a visit from Harriet. This week Dr Roberts brought Mr Harris,the surgeon, to see her and they talked about the proposed operations on her hips. Irene had heard all that Dr Roberts had to say about operations and she felt about them rather as she felt about the prospect of friendship with Harriet: she did not dare to hope. Sometimes her thoughts would race ahead to the day when she would be able to do this or that, but then she would quickly draw in the reins and tell herself it might not be like that. Dr Roberts annoyed her because he promised too much and she knew that he knew that there could be snags; she did not get on with him very well and she had never tried to explain to him that she wanted to hear the worst.

She had not met Mr Harris before and she knew some of the patients did not like him because of his abrupt manner. He looked very stern as he studied the X ray photographs of her hips. Then he looked up over the top of his glasses and said, 'You realize we can promise you nothing. You may not be able to walk any better or any further. You will have to learn how to walk all over again. This is easier said than done. Also, I hope you do not imagine that the new joints will be painless. We cannot promise that you will have any less pain than you have now.'

As soon as Irene was told there could be no promises she felt confident that all would go well for her; she was glad he had told her it was up to her to learn to walk because she was sure she would have the staying power to try again and again. 'I know you can't promise anything,' she said. 'But I want to have the operations all the same.'

He smiled very slightly when she said that and she knew that they understood one another.

When the doctors had gone Sister came and spoke to her. 'You mustn't let Mr Harris discourage you. He always talks like that, but he is a very clever surgeon and I have seen numberless patients of his make quite remarkable recoveries. But now I've got some good news for you,' she went on. 'Mrs Parr is so eager to go home that as soon as the doctor discharged her she rang up her husband and he is coming to fetch her this evening. So you can stay up for supper – you'll be moving into the next room as soon as she has gone, and into a low bed.'

So Irene had her supper in the dayroom with the other patients, looking out over the wide rolling country while the sun dipped slowly behind a distant belt of woodland. This is the real happy ending, she thought. Everything had changed. Now that she had spoken to Mr Harris her whole future appeared in a different light. And as a sign of it, her immediate life in the hospital had changed. She must still be more dependent on others than she would be at home, but the change after the last ten days was so great that she felt she had never tasted such freedom before. The ward consisted of several rooms along a corridor and she had now been moved into one of the smaller ones which had only four beds in it; the only other occupant was Miss Benstead, who had come into hospital that day. The next morning Birdie moved in to join them, while the fourth bed remained empty. There was no television.

Irene was pleased to find that she had been thrust into Miss Benstead's company, as she had felt an interest in her ever since Birdie had told her of her dislike of OT. But if Irene had hoped to make her acquaintance she was disappointed that first evening when they were alone together. Miss Benstead announced: 'I hope you won't be lonely in here. I don't talk much. I read.'

'I like to read too,' Irene hastily assured her. 'I'm so glad to get away from the television.' She took a covert look at the books Miss Benstead had on her locker and realized they were not the sort of books she herself read. She had somehow imagined she would find a kindred spirit in Miss Benstead and the sight of period novels with crinolined ladies on the dustjackets made her spirits sink. Miss Benstead had a habit of looking up from her book over the top of her reading glasses, without saying anything, which Irene found intimidating. When at last the book was laid aside Irene gathered all her courage to say, 'I'm glad I've met Mr Harris at last.'

At first she thought Miss Benstead was not going to answer her at all. She did not realize that over a lifetime of school-teaching Miss Benstead had acquired certain habits, one of which was this pause before she spoke; this made her utterances appear more weighty. 'Mr Harris always tells you the truth,' she said at last. 'He is the only person in this hospital who can afford to be honest because he is the only person who knows what he's talking about. Never attempt to ask the junior doctors what is going on. It is simply a waste of time, as they don't know themselves.' Having delivered herself of this speech she relapsed into silence once more.

Irene was relieved when Birdie joined them next morning. Birdie had a way with everyone. She and Miss Benstead had long since struck up an alliance because they both liked to have the window open. Miss Benstead always addressed Birdie as

Mrs Sparrow, and Irene discovered that she rose in Miss Benstead's estimation when she adopted this habit at least when referring to Birdie in the third person. Miss Benstead addressed the nurses as nurse, and despite her slighting reference to junior doctors she treated them with the respect due to their office. This insistence on decorum made her seem stiff and forbidding to begin with.

Yet Irene came to the conclusion in the end that Miss Benstead was shy. At first this seemed hardly likely. She had been not only a schoolmistress but for many years the headmistress of a small country school, an awe-inspiring figure amongst her pupils and in the whole local community. In hospital she had no rôle in the social structure. She was quite incapable of being matey. As soon as Birdie was there to act as intermediary she become kind and gracious to Irene and although she spent much of her time reading, they had plenty of conversation and Irene was fascinated to hear stories of school life told from the headmistress's point of view. Sometimes they were much racier than you might expect.

It was a different world in the small room, peaceful and companionable. Sometimes Birdie and Miss Benstead went back into the large room to watch some favoured programme on the television and then Irene could have the pleasure of complete solitude, though she felt less need of it now. It was when she was alone that she gazed out of the window. From this point of view rather further along the building, the 'little wood' had recomposed its ranks. She wondered if she could ever have thought it a wood if she had first seen it from here. She could even see one of the chimneys of the farmhouse through a gap in the trees. Her visit there had the dim unreality of a dream, disconnected from the ordinary course of her life, and she no more expected a repeat of it than she would have expected to dream a further instalment of a dream she had had. They had made wild promises but they would have forgotten about her by now.

Chapter X

So she was amazed when Harriet arrived on Sunday afternoon with the promised bookrest under her arm. 'I thought you might think we'd forgotten all about you,' said Harriet, 'so I came today to bring you this. You've been moved to a different room.'

Irene was delighted; yet also disquieted. She did not want them to press her to go over to the Glebe again. It was extraordinarily kind of Mr Pollard to have had the bookrest made for her, yet she wished he had let her alone. It was almost as if he were bullying her. 'You see they've found me a lower bed,' she said.

'Then you won't want the bookrest,' Harriet said flatly. Her disappointment made her look sulky.

Irene's contradictory feelings quickly resolved themselves. She felt irritated with Harriet who had so little imagination that she could not see how important this change of bed was to her. There was a testy note in her voice as she replied, 'What do you mean? Of course I want the bookrest. Show me how it works.'

As soon as Harriet began to set up the bookrest she lost her sulky look. Like Mr Pollard's harness, it was both very simple and yet incredibly ingenious. Harriet was eager to explain how it worked. Miss Benstead was watching her over the top of her glasses and Irene appealed to her. 'Mr Pollard has made it for me so that I can read while I'm lying in bed. Isn't it kind of him?'

Miss Benstead would never have barged in on another person's visitor without invitation, but she was really interested in the bookrest. 'Just what I've always wanted,' she said. 'You're a lucky girl.'

Harriet wanted to put a book in, to show how it was held in place and how the pages could be turned. She had stretched out her hand for one of the slim volumes of poetry, but Irene said, 'I don't need a bookrest for them. Try one of Miss Benstead's books – they're thicker than anything I've got.'

It was easy while the conversation remained between the three of them. Harriet was obviously proud of the bookrest on Mr Pollard's behalf, and delighted at Miss Benstead's admiration, which in its turn made Irene's gratitude seem more spontaneous and equal to the occasion. 'You must assure Mr Pollard that I really am grateful,' she said. 'But tell him too that hospital isn't quite so hopelessly disorganized as he supposes and that they actually have found me a lower bed. He'll know that I shall still want to use the bookrest a good deal. I can see I'll have to, or else Miss Benstead will quietly take it over.'

'His films haven't come back from processing,' said Harriet. 'As soon as they come, I'm to fetch you over.'

So there it was, the outside world, the world beyond the window, still expecting to impinge on her. She didn't want to go. She remembered how Sister had come to reassure her after Mr Harris had spoken to her and, although she did not need the reassurance, she had been touched by Sister's solicitude; and Sister had been so glad to announce that she could now be moved to a lower bed. Breaking the rules would be a poor way to repay kindness. But all she said to Harriet was, 'Go and look out of the window. You'll see what the Glebe looks like from inside the blot on the landscape. Didn't somebody say that the only place to see Paris was from the Eiffel Tower, because it's the only place from which you can't see the Eiffel Tower? We certainly get some magnificent views from inside this blot. To the west, if you take a peep in the dayroom, we look out over miles and miles of rolling country, as far as the eye can see. It looks as if it went on for ever.'

'When I was a child,' said Harriet, 'I thought it did go on

for ever. On the one side was the town, on the other the country. There are lots of green lanes that go out to the west and when my mother took me in the pushchair we never came to the end of the green lanes. If we went as far as Hayley woods, which was a great expedition in those days, it was as if we had reached the horizon and could see beyond it. And still the green lanes went on and it was country for ever. My mother doesn't think much of the country round here and she used to say, "One day we'll take you to see some real mountains. We'll take you to see the Lakes." I used to think if we went on long enough along the green lanes we would come to those fabulous mountains and the Lakes where people wrote poetry, or so she said. But we always turned back. We never went there.'

'Never?' said Irene.

'Oh, we went in the end,' said Harriet, 'by train. By then I knew that the green lanes didn't go on for ever. You come to the road. There's a petrol station. Of course there are more lanes beyond, but then you come to more suburban development. When I was a child Granstead wasn't yet a commuter dormitory – the railway was too far away. But now everyone has cars and every year more and more of the country disappears. When I walk along the green lanes I try to pretend the suburbs aren't there, but it's never the same as it used to be. Sometimes I get back a little of the old feeling just by saying the words "Over the hills and far away". It's a sort of spell, only I don't use it too often in case it wears out.'

'And the Lakes?'

'The Lakes were full of people when I got there,' said Harriet with disgust. 'The top of Helvellyn was like Piccadilly Circus and there were traffic jams on Striding Edge. You had to stop where it was wide to let people pass you. And there weren't any poets. I always had this stupid idea that these poets would be sort of supermen with shining eyes and hair floating in the wind.'

'So you read poetry,' said Irene thoughtfully.

'Not really,' said Harriet hastily. 'I just think it would be a nice idea if I did, and then I don't.' She blushed and looked at her hands. 'But you do: you said so.'

Most people Irene had met seemed to think that the reading of poetry was an intellectual affectation. At best it was tolerated, sometimes mocked, but worst of all people could think it implied an assumption of superiority which they resented.

'Look in my locker,' she said. 'You'll find a book there by Kathleen Raine. You've not read her? There's a poem in that book which begins:

> *I came too late to the hills.*
> *They were stripped bare*
> *Of song and story.*

I think you'd like that.'

Harriet had found the book. Her fingers were trembling as she searched for the place and Irene could see that she wanted to read the poem all at one gulp; she was too excited to read it word by word. 'Borrow it if you like,' she said. 'It belongs to my uncle but I don't suppose he'll mind. He's always trying to convert people to poetry.'

'Can I really?' said Harriet, overjoyed. 'I'll take great care of it. When I come to fetch you with the wonderful chair, I'll bring it back.'

But Irene had other plans. She wanted to persuade Harriet to come and visit her in hospital without taking her out. 'I think perhaps it would be better if I stayed inside the blot,' she said. 'Quite apart from rules, I'm learning to bear it inside here. It'll only turn everything topsy-turvy for me if I go out.'

Harriet looked up from the book in surprise. 'I was just planning all sorts of outings,' she said, disappointed. 'I thought I could take you along the green lanes as my mother used to take me as a child and for you the countryside would go on for ever because we would never go as far as the road . . .'

'I can see I shall have to lend you some more poetry,' said Irene, 'only you've probably read *Fern Hill*.' She wanted to talk about something else so as to put off the question of going out.

'I tell you, I haven't read anything,' said Harriet. 'You must tell me what I ought to read.'

'I haven't got it here,' said Irene, seeing her eyes scanning the books on the locker, 'and I don't know it by heart. It was only that you wanted to recapture the country of your childhood through me, and I thought of the words "forever fled from the childless land", but I don't suppose that means anything out of context.'

'If you're afraid I'd only come once and then leave you in the lurch, I promise I won't do that,' said Harriet. 'We'd make it a regular thing and you'd always have something to look forward to while you were stuck in here.'

Irene sighed. 'I'm afraid I must seem a frightful stick-in-the-mud,' she said. 'It's difficult to explain to someone who doesn't belong to the world of hospital. These people are kind to me. I depend on them for so much. So you see I feel I have to co-operate and keep the rules just while I'm in here. I'd love to see you again. You could take me out in the gardens – that is allowed. But I'm afraid it wouldn't be much fun for you.'

'But of course it would be fun,' said Harriet. 'Perhaps I could bring you some books. I've suddenly started reading these holidays. It's all because of Ian. I don't think he reads poetry much, or anyway he's never mentioned any. But he's always mentioning books and I've never read them, so I have to rush straight to the library and get them out. You might like to read some of them too, except that you've probably read them before. They're mostly big heavy books, so you'll have to make use of the bookrest. It'll come in handy.'

'Who's this Ian?' asked Irene.

'Ian Pollard,' explained Harriet.

Irene suddenly remembered how Mavis had said, 'She do spend a lot of time down the Glebe these days.'

She asked, 'You see a lot of Mr Pollard?'

'He's coaching me in maths,' said Harriet quickly. 'I just have to get O level maths and I failed it for the third time this summer.'

'Then these are mathematical books?' said Irene quizzically.

'No, no – they're just books he happens to mention. He comes to supper with us several times a week because my mother

77

thinks he isn't feeding himself properly. Actually he talks to my father much more than he talks to me.'

'But you read every book that he mentions.'

'You see, I'd hardly read anything before,' Harriet blurted out. 'I don't know what I did do – just daydreamed I suppose, about this splendid poet with shining eyes and floating hair who was going to walk into my life and be so impressed by my poetic sensibility.'

'And instead it was Mr Pollard.'

Harriet blushed, then looked her straight in the eye and said, 'I suppose so.' Not to dwell on the subject she added quickly, 'So I can come and fetch you, can't I?'

Wearily, Irene began all over again with her explanation of why she couldn't go out, but suddenly all her good reasons seemed to have dissolved away. Instead she found herself saying, 'Some days are out of the question because we have occupational therapy – that's on Mondays and Wednesdays. And on Thursdays the specialists come . . .'

'So you will come after all!' Harriet looked delighted.

'I oughtn't to,' said Irene regretfully. But she no longer meant it.

Afterwards she wondered why she had let herself be persuaded. The country walks had sounded delightful, but she had not weakened then. The point at which she had changed her mind was when Harriet was talking about her 'Ian'. (Irene still thought of him as Mr Pollard and when she said 'Ian' to herself she put it between inverted commas.) Hearing him spoken of, she forgot her dislike of him and felt a sudden envy of Harriet who had some chance of knowing what he was really like. They all had their loves – Linda, Eileen, Harriet; it seemed all life went on in the world outside, the world beyond the window, and she was destined never to play a part in it:

> *She hath no loyal knight and true*
> *The Lady of Shalott.*

Remembering the poem, she felt a shiver of dread. What had she done? Would the curse now fall on her? She wondered

78

about the 'insurance' of which Mavis had spoken. Insurance against what? In case she should have an accident? Of course it would be wiser to stay inside the hospital grounds, but would she dare tell Harriet that she had changed her mind again? Perhaps it would rain and then they wouldn't be able to go. But when she envisaged such a possibility she realised how much she wanted to go.

Chapter XI

IT had been Eileen's weekend off and when she came back on the Monday she was bubbling over with her own affairs. A number of friends had gone on a boating trip and she had contrived to fall into the water, but Terry had declined to jump in and rescue her; he pointed out that she could perfectly well swim to safety. Afterwards she looked a fright and the whole afternoon was spoiled; Terry would do nothing but tease her. But in the evening he repented and danced with her, so all her sorrows were wiped out in a dream of delight.

When the convoy set off for OT Eileen whispered to Irene, 'Shall I take you out into the garden instead?'

'Not today,' said Irene. 'I'll explain why later. I've got something to tell you.'

When they had come back from OT she managed to get Eileen to herself and said, 'I don't think I'd better skip OT. After last week's drama they are sure to notice if I go missing and I don't want to blot my copybook, because tomorrow a friend of mine is coming and she is going to take me out – outside the grounds, I mean.'

'Sister'll never give you permission,' said Eileen.

'Of course not,' said Irene. 'We'll go down into the garden and then we'll just quietly slip away. We're only going for a little country walk, nothing very exciting, but for me it will be like going onto another planet, just to get away from this place.'

'I don't know why they don't let patients go out,' said Eileen. 'What harm would it do? In the men's wards they get up to all sorts of things and nobody ever comes to any harm. But Sister still thinks she's in charge of a prison, practically.'

'Isn't it something to do with insurance?'

'That's what they say. If you was a surgical case I'd understand. You have to be careful of infection and you wouldn't want to have an accident with a new joint. But after all, you're no different from what you are at home, and you go out when you're living at home. If you had an accident — with a car or something — you wouldn't sue the hospital, would you?'

Irene shook her head. 'So you don't think I'm frightfully wicked?'

'Lord no! Nobody'll say a word to Sister. If you slip away down the back drive, who's going to see you?'

Irene did not mention anything about the wonderful chair — in fact she had forgotten about it. When Harriet came to fetch her the next day, Eileen caught a glimpse of the chair and was overcome by curiosity. She had not meant to take more than a distant interest in Irene's friend, scarcely expecting to be introduced, but as soon as she saw the chair she guessed it must be of Mr Pollard's making. There had been a lot of talk about his inventions amongst the hospital staff, but Eileen had never seen any of them before. She followed Harriet into the room and stood staring at the chair from the doorway.

She was not the only one. Quite a crowd gathered — several nurses and one or two patients from the other rooms. Harriet paraded the chair. She put a shoe in its way and showed how the wheel gave to it, mounted it and went on, all in a smooth motion without a jolt.

'We caused quite a stir,' said Harriet when they were at last going down in the lift.

Irene was not too pleased to have attracted so much attention just when she had hoped to slip away unseen. 'Perhaps it would have been wiser to leave the wonderful chair downstairs and pick it up on route,' she said. 'But it can't be helped now. So long as they none of them suspect that we are going beyond the gardens it's all right. You shouldn't have said that about rough country.'

Irene was horrified when they emerged from the lift on the ground floor and found Sister waiting to go up. But Sister was all smiles. 'I'm so glad you've got a visitor to take you out into the garden on a lovely day like this,' she said. She held open the fire door to let them pass through. There was a moment's confusion as Harriet had been going to dive straight down the passage opposite the lift, the back way that Mavis had taken.

'We turn to the right,' said Irene.

'Oh, I thought,' began Harriet, but did as she was told.

Sister had by now noticed the chair. 'Did you bring that with you?' she asked Harriet.

'Yes.'

'I thought for a moment it was a chair made by one of our patients,' said Sister.

'It *is* the chair made by Mr Pollard,' said Irene. 'My friend knows him.'

Sister looked at Harriet with a frown. 'You live locally?' she asked.

'Yes,' admitted Harriet, discomforted by the frown.

'That will be very nice for Ireen,' said Sister. 'You must come and see her often.' She smiled graciously and went back to the lift. The patients at Granstead came from a very wide catchment area so that few of them could expect many visits from their friends and relations and Sister was pleased that Irene had found a friend in the locality.

Because she felt guilty, Irene had expected the worst. From moment to moment she had imagined Sister would suspect something. That frowning scrutiny to which she had subjected Harriet was worst of all; Sister had only been thinking 'Have I seen this girl before?' but to Irene it seemed that she had already guessed their plans.

They were out in the gardens now, in the sunshine, amongst beds of lobelia and salvia. 'Pretend we're just strolling around,' said Irene. 'We'll see if we can find a way through to the back drive down the far end of the building. We don't want to go the way Mavis brought us amongst the dustbins and bicycle sheds – it would look far too suspicious.'

They wandered about in silence for a little while until they found a path through the shrubbery which took them where they wanted to go. Irene broke the silence by asking, 'And what books has Mr Pollard been mentioning lately?'

'Ian?' Irene could not see Harriet's face, but from a slight increase in velocity she guessed that her heart had leapt up at the mention of his name. She seemed to dwell on the thought of it for a moment or two and then she said hurriedly, 'You won't tell him I read every book he mentions, will you?'

'But don't you talk to him about the books you're reading?' asked Irene in surprise.

'It doesn't somehow seem to come up in everyday conversation,' said Harriet.

'But you say he's always mentioning books in everyday conversation.'

'Yes, but when he mentions them I haven't read them, and when I've read them, he mentions something else that I haven't read.'

'I don't see why you can't bring them up in conversation yourself.'

'I wish I could,' said Harriet, 'but, you see, then he might guess . . .'

'Guess what? that you're in love with him?'

Harriet laughed. Once more she was pushing the chair at a great pace.

'You don't want him to know that you're in love with him?' asked Irene.

'You won't tell him – please don't tell him!' begged Harriet. 'When he first came, I couldn't stop talking about him. At home I kept on bringing him up. Everything that happened, everything that anyone said, seemed to lead to him. I was just waiting the whole time for an opportunity to mention his name. Then my father said this thing. He said, "You've got a crush on Ian Pollard." So after that I stopped talking about him. I only hope he never told him. I should die of shame.'

Irene considered the offensive word.

'Of course I know I'm just infatuated with him,' said Harriet defensively.

'But it's made a big difference to you? It's changed your life?' said Irene thoughtfully.

'Sometimes I think I was hardly alive before!'

'Then what does it matter what we call it? Crush – infatuation – love. It's an emotion that's changed your life, so why be ashamed of it? You're lucky – nothing like that will ever happen to me.'

Harriet did not contradict her. Just at this point she lowered her voice and said, 'Take a look at the wishing well in the garden on the right and tell me what you think of it.'

'It's incredible,' said Irene. 'But Mavis told me it belonged to her nephew Neil.'

'Yes,' said Harriet. 'He was brought up at Glebe Cottage, but now he has wall-to-wall carpets and a wishing well in his garden. He and Ian get on ever so well. Neil even thinks they could go into business together, producing things like your bookrest.'

'I suppose Ian Pollard will go back to work for that aircraft firm when he's well enough,' said Irene.

'I don't know – I think that the accident has changed his whole attitude to life.' Harriet was torn between the desire to talk about Ian Pollard and the dread of talking too much about him. She interrupted herself to say, 'That's where I live.'

'Stop a moment,' said Irene. 'I want to see.'

'It's only a very ordinary suburban house. It used to be right out in the country. We looked out over fields, like I told you, and the cows grazed here in the days when the Glebe was a dairy farm. You see what they've called the estate' – she pointed out the street sign – ' "Greenfields". Once it really was green fields. In those days there was only the hospital.'

'A blot on the landscape.'

'My mother used to call it the eyesore. When I was little I thought that was its proper name. Do you know, I'd never been inside it till I took you back last week?'

'I'm not surprised. I always get the feeling in hospital that we've been "put away". There's no connection with the outside world.'

'I think that's what Ian felt. That's why he asked Mavis if she could find him lodgings so that he only had to go into the hospital for treatment.'

'I envy him,' said Irene. 'He's got his workshop. He's not condemned to occupational therapy. He can do something worthwhile while he's having treatment.'

'Ah, but that's his problem. Does he find it worthwhile?'

'That bookrest was very worthwhile as far as I'm concerned.'

'But perhaps not as far as he's concerned,' said Harriet. 'You see, he says he doesn't want to go back to designing aircraft – he doesn't know how he ever lent himself to that capitalist ramp. On the other hand he says, "I mustn't fall into the error of doing good. I only do this work because it keeps me occupied for the time being." '

'The error of doing good?' said Irene. 'I've never heard that before. The more good deeds we have, the better, I think.'

> 'How far that little candle throws his beams!
> So shines a good deed in a naughty world,'

quoted Harriet.

'I thought you told me you hadn't read any poetry,' said Irene. 'Where does that come from?'

'The Merchant of Venice,' said Harriet. She was so pleased to have produced a quotation that she decided not to spoil the effect by admitting she had played the part of Portia in the school production. Perhaps this might have stirred Irene's memory. As it was, the old world of school which Clare and Diana had tried to recall to her seemed so remote from her present reality that she did not make the connection. 'I think that what Ian means is that some people do good because it makes them feel good and often they're doing more harm than good. He thinks there are people like that at the hospital.'

'Oh, does he?' said Irene, immediately on the defensive. 'Well, I can only say that I'm very grateful that there are some people with enough love in their hearts to nurse me and others like me, and I don't mind if it does make them feel good.'

'I've explained it all wrong,' said Harriet. 'It sounds quite different when he's talking.'

'He seems to have told you a lot about himself.'

'He talks to my father – I told you so before. He doesn't talk about these things to me. He comes over to supper at least three times a week because otherwise he doesn't feed himself properly. Do you know what he eats all the time? Pork pie and cream buns. "It's what I like," he says, "and it's very simple. Why should one eat something different every day? Children are wiser than we are," he says, "because they'd be quite happy to eat their favourite food all the time." He eats apples, too – but he won't eat oranges because you can't do anything else while you're eating an orange.'

'I think there's something very sad about your Ian,' said Irene. 'He's all negative. He can't eat an orange for its own sake, nor invent things for the sake of other people.'

Harriet, for whom everything Ian Pollard said or did had a charm of its own, considered this extraneous opinion. 'Perhaps so,' she said unwillingly.

They went into the house by the back door. There was a large flagged kitchen, hardly furnished at all, except for a huge table covered with oilcloth and a wooden settle. The Busbys had left some furniture behind when they went, the big stuff which wouldn't fit into their bungalow.

'He has a water bed – perhaps Mavis has told you,' said Harriet. 'She's sure he'll wake up one day half drowned and soaked to the skin. It's in there, where Mr Busby had his office. He doesn't go upstairs at all and he doesn't use the other ground floor rooms, except today, for showing the films.'

They crossed a passage and came into a large room filled with dim light. The shutters were closed, but sunlight came in round the edges; honey-suckle had also crept in, anaemic but hopeful, clutching at an old curtain rail. The room had a smell of long disuse. Wallpaper, which had been scribbled on at the bottom, hung away from the walls. At one point the wallpaper had been torn away and lay in a heap in the corner.

'We tried to make a smooth surface to project the picture on to,' said Ian Pollard, 'without much success. I ought to have had my screen sent down here, but I thought I could do without it.'

'It'll just be one more factor to turn us poor cripples into a surrealist happening,' said Irene. 'I've often thought it would make a macabre film – the scene of us in the wobbly water with all our deformities revealed.'

'You think of making films?' he asked.

'I don't make anything. I'm just an observer. I don't think I've got the imagination to create anything, and anyway it's too difficult as things are.'

'At least you know what you're going to see,' he said. 'Poor Harriet got a nasty shock. She lives under the shadow of the hospital but she had never noticed rheumatoid arthritis before.'

Strangely, Irene was horrified by the film too. She forced herself to watch it several times, and in slow motion, so that she could explain what further support she needed in the harness, but she was very relieved when they turned to the film of herself in the chair. It amused her to watch Harriet pushing her. It was something she had not been able to see at the time, both because she was in the chair and because she knew nothing of Harriet's feelings. Poor Harriet, sent off to take the cripple for a jaunt, while Mavis stayed behind to set up the camera for the man she admired! No wonder she had been so uncommunicative. There she was, walking up and down in front of him, looking at him, smiling, deliberately not looking at him. Irene paid little attention to the action of the wonderful wheels; she was too intent on the human drama. Besides, it was a relief to watch someone whole in every limb, graceful and easy in movement.

When it was over she said, 'I thought I was going to escape from the hospital for the afternoon. Somehow, when I'm part of it I take it so much for granted. But suddenly to see it as the camera sees it, objectively – that's a very different thing.'

'I'm sorry,' said Ian Pollard. 'Harriet must take you out into the fresh air. She must show you the garden.'

'There's no need to be sorry,' said Irene. 'I hadn't expected to feel like that. I suppose I hate having to look at other cripples. I should like to live surrounded by athletes. Last year I went to a holiday camp for cripples. Oh, the well-meaning jollity, the wheelchair races . . . we were supposed to enjoy being all-cripples-together.'

'I'm sure they didn't call you cripples,' said Ian Pollard. 'Like our friend Miss Howell, they probably found it a dirty word. I never know quite what people hope to achieve by calling things by different names.'

It was something she might have said herself, but Irene suddenly felt her indignation rising. 'There *are* people who don't like being called cripples,' she said sharply. 'You and I aren't exactly typical. Lots of people enjoyed that camp. I don't want to criticize them and I don't want to criticize the people who ran it. It just happened to be wrong for me. Other people may be happier in the company of those who have the same handicaps as themselves.' She stopped abruptly, wondering why she felt so irritated with him. 'It would be nice to see the garden,' she said, 'if Harriet doesn't mind.'

When they were outside Harriet said, 'You do get fierce with him.'

'I'm sorry. I've dragged you away. You can just leave me if you like, and go and help him put away the projector.'

But Harriet shook her head. 'I see plenty of him and I don't see much of you. Besides, I never have much to say to him. I'd never dare talk to him like that. I wish I could.'

'I suppose I find him too like myself,' said Irene. 'I see all my faults in him.'

Chapter XII

When the first outing with Harriet had gone off without mishap, Irene began to feel less nervous. Nobody had suspected that they went beyond the gardens. Some of the other patients used to go down to the garden, if they had visitors to take them or were mobile enough to go by themselves, but they all kept fairly close to the building, sunning themselves amongst the flower beds. The grounds were large and no one considered it odd that the two girls should disappear down a remote corner. In some parts the grass had been grown for hay and the going was very rough, but they had the wonderful chair. The chair continued to attract attention but roused no suspicions, except Eileen's.

Eileen knew Irene had not told her everything. She did not guess at that first outing with Mavis but she knew something had been kept in reserve, and she did guess that Irene had met Mr Pollard. Irene had been going to avoid mentioning him; she described to Eileen the walk round to the Glebe, but if she thought she could limit herself to descriptions of nature she was much mistaken. Eileen listened to all this without much interest and then burst out, 'And what's Mr Pollard like? What did you think of him?'

Irene was never one to tell the whole truth, but she did not like telling deliberate lies so she began to describe his appearance. 'He's middle-aged, you know – he has grey hair, rather pale grey eyes, bushy eyebrows. He wears glasses . . .'

'Yes, I know,' said Eileen. 'I've seen him myself. I wanted to know what he was like to talk to – you know what I mean.'

'I haven't really had much chance to talk to him,' said Irene. Eileen was dissatisfied. 'I should've thought you could've told me a bit about him,' she said, but did not press the point. She knew Irene came from a different world from her own. 'Toffs are like that,' she thought, without rancour. 'They like to keep themselves to themselves.'

Irene found it more difficult to bear the petty irritations of hospital life now she had had a taste of freedom. The windows of the OT room looked out over the garden. She sat idly with her task before her, gazing out. It was another glorious hot summer's afternoon. A shimmer of heat rose from the asphalt of the front drive and there were dark pools of shadow under the evergreens. Other people were free to come and go. A car drove up to the front entrance and a girl leapt out and ran up the steps. A moment later she reappeared, laughing and talking to someone who had come out of the building with her. She got back into the car – the engine was still running – and drove away, going from sunlight to shadow, sunlight to shadow, down the avenue of trees that led to the outside world. To Irene she was a symbol of the liberty other people enjoyed who were not compelled to wind string round nails. She was sick with the desire to go out, to be free. If she had been honest she would have known that it was her condition that kept her a prisoner, but the mood was upon her to blame everything on the hospital once more. They forced her to go to occupational therapy. They had stupid rules about not leaving the grounds. If only she could have come as an outpatient, like Mr Pollard. But Mavis had told her, and she had heard it before, that Miss Howell didn't like outpatients. How typical! She forgot that she had wanted to give her mother a holiday; she forgot how long the daily drive to the hospital would be; she saw only that they wanted to keep her neatly filed under their control. As she was already breaking the rules it was necessary for her to believe that the rules and the institution that made them were senseless and intolerable. All her good resolutions were forgotten.

On the Friday Harriet came for her again. They were to go on a walk down the green lanes, but first Ian Pollard wanted to see Irene.

'He seems to have taken quite a fancy to you,' said Harriet, looking pleased because it meant she would be one of the party. 'He wants to talk to you about things at the hospital.'

Irene imagined he must have something in particular that he wanted to ask her, but this was not the case. She kept expecting a question which never came. It appeared Ian Pollard was on friendly terms with some of the junior physiotherapists and they came over to the Glebe to pick his brains and to grumble about their superiors.

'Physiotherapy is something which is changing all the time,' he said. 'There is new equipment which they could have in the gym, which did not even exist three or four years ago. But those like our friend Miss Howell think that what was good enough when they trained ought to be good enough for the next generation.'

Irene wanted changes in the hospital, yet something about Ian Pollard antagonized her. He was only a newcomer and he was too ready to criticize; Mrs Chandler was one of his chief allies and Irene could not forget how she had treated her as no more than a name on a list. 'It's a change of attitude we want, not a change of equipment,' she said. 'They'd treat our bodies all right if they once thought that we, as people, were not accidental and inconvenient appendages which unfortunately had to accompany the said bodies into hospital. You'd like to reduce it all to mechanics – yet you yourself couldn't stand being hospitalized. Miss Howell doesn't like outpatients. Most of us live too far away to come as outpatients anyway, but even if we lived down the road she'd prefer to have us incarcerated so that our bodies would be readily available to her in an orderly controlled situation. It never occurs to her that body and soul are one and that she can't cure the body as long as she insists on reducing people to helpless invalids, to numbers on a list.'

Several times he had tried to interrupt her, but she forged on, finding an outlet for her renewed sense of rebellion in attacking him. 'You've no reason to suppose that I think it's all a matter of mechanics,' he said in a hurt voice when she had finished, 'or even that I think the mechanics is the most important part. I think I understand as well as you that you can't divide up a human being. I know from personal experience that you've got to have the will to get better and "hospitalization" — horrid word! but what they've done to the word is what they do to people in hospital — hospitalization can destroy the will to get better. All right?'

Irene was ashamed of the vehemence of her attack. She had never expected him to sound hurt. 'I'm sorry,' she said. 'I had no right to say that.'

He smiled. 'Of course I *am* interested in the mechanics — I'm a mechanic, and it's the field in which I can most usefully intervene. After all it must play a large part in *physio*therapy — occupational therapy is there to look after the whole man.'

'Occupational therapy!' Irene exploded again. 'What have basket-work and making those hideous things with string got to do with the whole man? Rather the reverse — they treat us like children, giving us something useless to do to keep us out of mischief.'

He was silent a moment. 'It's not meant to be like that,' he said. 'Those hideous things with string, as you call them — I got out of making one of them by offering to drive in the nails for other people. I even invented some new patterns! Can you forgive me that?'

'You're lucky,' she said. 'You can do so much with your hands. You have the satisfaction of being able to make yourself useful.'

'It was OT gave me that satisfaction by giving me something to do, and so I'm grateful to them. You see, however hideous and pointless those things are, I'm grateful that somebody made me do something at that time. An awful inertia came over me in hospital. You must know what I mean — I see it happening to everyone around me. They've been ill, had an operation or whatever, but now they're better and could be doing all sorts of things, but somehow they can't bestir themselves. It doesn't help anyone to lounge around lethargically. You've got to behave as if you were well before you can get well.'

This was the very argument to appeal to Irene, but somehow she could not connect it with OT. 'But all those things we do are so useless . . .' she began.

'I know,' he interrupted her. 'OT is very limited as practised here. Arts and crafts are all very well, but there is so much more we could be doing. Old Miss Miles is a dear – I won't hear anything against her – but she's dreadfully behind the times. Did you know in some hospitals you can cook for OT? Or there's gardening or carpentry, but you'd be surprised how many men choose to cook. An able-bodied man doesn't mind if his wife does everything for him, but a cripple hates being dependent, just because he has to be. That's something I've learnt since I've been in hospital.'

'You can cook in OT? But that's sensible,' exclaimed Irene. 'Lots of women are afraid they won't be able to cope when they get home. They'd like to keep in practice and show off their private recipes at the same time.'

'I'll tell you something else that you'd approve of – Meg Chandler was telling me that in one of these arthritis hospitals in Norfolk they have a self-contained flat where patients can live and try looking after themselves while they are still having treatment. That's all part of OT. I was saying that they ought to buy up this farmhouse and run it as a hostel where patients could have a measure of independence.'

'But that's a marvellous idea!' said Irene.

'I thought it would appeal to you,' he said. 'But what really interests me is the "mechanical" side – I'd like to see an experimental kitchen in OT where the height of every surface would be adjustable – and the height of stoves and sinks and fridges too. Then people could discover just how best things could be arranged for them at home. Most of them have some trick or gadget which they find invaluable. They could pool ideas and think up new ones. The hospital workshop could send them home with all sorts of useful aids. This isn't my own idea, I humbly submit – it is actually being tried in some places – but it's the sort of scheme I should love to have a hand in. So you see, OT can equip us for independence outside the hospital, and independence is what the whole man needs. That's what I meant when I said OT was there to look after the whole man.'

Irene always went to extremes and occupational therapy, as he explained it, won her enthusiastic support. Unfortunately this only made her feel the more aggrieved with the OT department at Granstead; there was so much they could have done for her and they didn't. 'I feel so helpless,' she complained. 'I've never cooked – was ill too young. I can never be independent.'

'Cooking's easy,' he assured her. 'Just wait till you've had your operations. Then I'll design you the ideal kitchen for your needs.'

'I don't know what I've done to deserve such kindness,' she said. 'But I don't think it would work out, you know, because of my mother. I mean, I can't see her ever letting me cook at home and I don't see how I could go off and live by myself when I've never had any practice looking after myself. Anyway, how would I earn my living?'

'We'll have to re-educate your mother,' he said. 'She can't expect to keep you as a child for ever. Sometimes real love is best shown in a willingness to let go.'

'You don't realize how difficult it is for her,' said Irene. She felt her anger rising in defence of her mother. In a strange way his wildly generous offer of designing a kitchen made her feel threatened. He wanted to take over her life.

'She must be plain unreasonable if she won't let you cook,' he said.

Irene kept a tight grip on her temper. 'Maybe she would let me – maybe I'm wrong,' she said. 'But all the same it would be one long battle. It's her kitchen, her empire. Things would have to be altered to make it possible for me. And I'd drive her mad, doing things so slowly.'

'If she loves you she'll be ready to sacrifice her temporary convenience to giving you a chance of having a life of your own.'

'Of course my mother loves me,' said Irene, her voice rising shrilly. 'Have you never loved anyone in all your life that you don't know it's not as simple as all that? I'm sorry,' she went on, feeling instantly deflated, 'but I don't think you've any right to criticize my mother whom you've never even met.'

He was silent and she felt forced to repeat her apology. 'I'm sorry.'

'I'm sorry too,' he said. 'I didn't mean to criticize your mother. Let's forget we ever had any disagreement. Harriet's longing to take you out – make sure you enjoy yourself.'

Harriet set off with the wonderful chair on their first country walk. Irene was still feeling churned up and unsettled by her own uncalled-for outburst, but the motion seemed to calm her; just as, when the train stops at a station we are restless and impatient, but as soon as it starts again our thoughts flow on in company with the everchanging scene beyond the window. Irene wondered if it was just because she had to spend so much of her life stationary that she always worried at the same thoughts, never able to dismiss stale problems from her mind. She did not know why she was so perverse with Ian Pollard but the passage of the trees and hedges past her eyes began to claim her attention. Make sure you enjoy yourself, he had said. That was not difficult.

Irene had never been for a walk like this before. Her mother did so much for her but she did not normally take her for walks unless there was some specific end in view; they went to church and to visit friends. Her father's outings were gratuitous, but they were always in the car. It was very different to be inside the landscape so that she felt part of it, not just an observer behind a screen. Besides, this was a landscape that she knew well as a distant prospect and to be amongst the familiar trees and hedges made her feel as if she herself had been transformed, as if she had drunk from the bottle called Drink Me and had succeeded in getting into the beautiful garden behind the door at the end of the dark passage like a rat hole. She was not her same self who sat at the window watching the whole landscape all knitted up by distance, when she followed the green lanes unravelling before her. Sometimes they came to a landmark that she knew well from the hospital: the little square house with a monkey-puzzle tree beside it turned up suddenly where two lanes met, with a dog barking furiously at the gate, amongst big bushes of fuchsia. In the evening, from the dayroom, she discovered that its identity had shifted. Hayley wood was much further away than she had expected, and larger too; when they got there it was no longer the horizon and a new landscape opened out beyond.

Harriet hated meeting people on these walks, finding solitude more poetic, and she was surprised to find Irene did not share this feeling. It was something which had always been taken for granted in her family, that landscape was spoiled if anyone else was there enjoying it. Other trippers made a trip vulgar. Irene simply preferred a landscape with figures and she was glad to be doing what other people did. She was delighted to meet small boys cutting themselves sticks from the hedges or trying to knock down unripe conkers. After her first surprise, Harriet began to reconsider her opinions. After all, here was someone who actually read poetry. Before long she had discovered that small boys had a picturesque charm wholly appropriate to the landscape. She had to discover the same thing about middle-aged ladies out walking their dogs, and about troops of girls riding on ponies. It was not that she had no opinions of her own, just that she had never examined them before.

Harriet was in the midst of a revolution and she had to see everything anew. In reality she knew little of Ian Pollard's opinions. In his presence she was abashed and could find nothing to say for herself. In every book that she read she tried to find him, to reconstruct his view of life, but often she had very little to go on, sometimes just a passing reference to an incident in the book, which didn't necessarily mean that he endorsed everything else that the author said. Sometimes Irene tired of these endless speculations on what his opinions might be, and she sighed when the hero of yet another book turned out to be 'like Ian'. 'Why don't you ask him what he thinks?' she asked.

Harriet pulled a face. 'I wish I was like you. I don't seem to be able to talk about these things properly.'

'But you talk about them all the time.'

'I don't mind talking about them to you. I know you won't laugh at me. I wish I could talk to Ian the way you do. When he says something I disagree with I can't think of any argument against it.'

'He and I always seem to be at cross purposes,' said Irene. 'I don't see any virtue in that.'

'He likes you all the same. Even when you rap him over the knuckles, as he calls it.'

'If he likes people to disagree with him, then try it yourself.'

'But I don't know how. I'm too ignorant.'

'I'm just as ignorant. I wish I didn't have to argue with him every time he opens his mouth. Sometimes I think that, if I had given him a chance to express himself, he might not have sounded quite as stupid as I thought.'

Harriet was always afraid of boring Irene with her obsession, but often it was Irene herself who came back to the subject. She could not ignore Ian Pollard. That weekend their meetings with him were rather brief, as they went on long walks together, and on Saturday they had tea with Harriet's parents and on Sunday at Glebe Cottage. Irene was glad of the opportunity to hear another opinion on Ian Pollard and questioned Harriet's parents about him, much to Harriet's delight, as she loved to hear him spoken of, but had denied herself this pleasure since her father had accused her of having a crush.

'I don't know what we shall do without him when he goes,' said Harriet's father. 'Granstead is a dead-alive sort of place and it has been a pleasure to have some civilized conversation.'

Her mother was more concerned about his welfare. 'He talks as if he didn't intend to go back to his job, even when he is well enough to do so. But I'm afraid that if he doesn't get back quickly to a normal pattern of life he will end by having some sort of nervous breakdown.'

'Nonsense,' protested her husband, 'he's better balanced than most people I know.'

Irene asked if they thought he was likely to go on with the work for the disabled.

Harriet's father replied, 'It's basically the *work* he's interested in, not the people it's done for. I think he should be able to work free lance and make contributions in many different fields.'

At Glebe Cottage Mr Pollard was less valued as a neighbour. Indeed, there was some feeling against him, because of his influence over Neil, whose mother feared that her boy might be induced to join Mr Pollard in some hare-brained enterprise. 'Them folks can afford to take risks, but folks like us don't have nothing to fall back on,' she said.

Though hardly aware of it, Irene had a basic desire to think ill of Ian Pollard and from all these sources she gleaned what she could to feed this antagonism. Harriet's mother thought he was unbalanced, Harriet's father had said he was not interested in people; he was willing to speculate in another person's livelihood. She imagined she was being shrewd in making these deductions from the odd word let slip; she forgot that her wiser self had sometimes wanted to be just to him.

The last outing they made that weekend was the one to Glebe Cottage on Sunday afternoon. Mavis's brother Bob had cut down all the mullein in preparation for their visit. 'Why it's only an old weed that'll grow up again quick enough,' he said. 'It were time I cleared that path anyway.'

The cottage when they reached it was, as Harriet had said, nothing much to look at. It was a bleak little box of yellow-grey brick with a slate roof, and so cramped inside that at first it seemed that they would never get the wonderful chair in. Mavis lived with her sister, Mrs Peacey, the mother of Neil and the widow of a brief wartime marriage, and her brother Bob. Whereas Mavis was long and bony Mrs Peacey was wide, like a huge cushion, almost too wide to go in at the door of Glebe Cottage. A sight to be seen on a bicycle, Harriet told Irene.

At home Mavis was only a minor figure. Her sister was head of the family and treated Mavis as if she was someone in need of care and protection. 'She lets herself be put upon,' said Mrs Peacey. This was with reference to Mr Pollard, but Irene felt it might equally apply to herself.

When there was difficulty getting the wonderful chair inside the house, Irene would have been quite happy to be served outside. She had almost obtained Mavis's consent to this when she realized that she would bring down the wrath of Mrs Peacey upon poor Mavis's head if she did not allow herself to be fitted into the chinese puzzle round the specially laid table in the front parlour. There were only vegetables in the garden apart from a few asters along the path – hardly a place for a lady to eat her tea. Perhaps Mrs Peacey had never noticed the view; it was just barns, fields and trees to her. 'Not like our Neil,' she said, 'he's made his garden really pretty.'

On the way back to the hospital Harriet would have liked to mock every item of the decor. Irene agreed at first, but soon tired of the game. 'They like it like that, so what?' she said. 'It's a room which tells a story, even if it is bad art. And because that story is Mavis's story I can even find it beautiful.'

Chapter XIII

SHE was sorry she had allowed herself to get irritated with Harriet on that last journey back. The weekend had sped past. Now it was all over. There was OT on Monday. Even while they were walking back the sun went in and, looking up, she realized that the sky had clouded over. The end of the fine weather, she thought. As always in hospital, she was prone to sudden fits of depression; when her excitement was snuffed out, utter blackness closed in. She tried to remind herself how lucky she was to be in the small room with the low bed; but that had only been bliss when it still stood in contrast to the big ward and going to bed at half past four. You get used to anything, good or bad. She had got used to going out and the prospect of whole days spent in hospital hit her with renewed force.

It was not until she met Harriet's parents that Irene discovered she and Harriet had been at the same school and even then she did not remember that Clare and Diana had mentioned her. Back in the ward that memory came to her suddenly and with a vividness that transported her back to the moment when the two of them had been speaking of a certain Hatty Moss who had played Portia, whose name and identity had held so little interest for her; she was astonished to realize that everything had changed for her in that short space of time. Then, the world beyond that window had been unattainable, unknown; all her hopes had been set on the far off day of her release from hospital. Now, when she reminded herself that it was barely two weeks to that release, the thought brought no joy; it was strange how remote home had become after this long period inside; the little world of Harriet and Ian Pollard now seemed the only reality outside the hospital walls and she felt a pang when she realized that going home would remove her for ever from their orbit. Just when she had met new people, just when she had made friends for the first time in her adult life, she was likely to be snatched away from them for ever.

If it rained she would never see Ian Pollard again, though Harriet might come, as she had promised, to visit her. She needed to see Ian Pollard again. The turmoil of hostile thoughts she had allowed herself to entertain could only be sent packing by his presence. She knew he would surprise her by being quite other than she expected and yet she could not conjure up in her mind's eye the real positive person to replace the shadow cast by her own hostility.

That night at supper Mrs Boundy was full of innuendo. 'Some people seem to be having a good time,' she said with one of her monstrous winks. At first Irene hardly realized that this referred to her and did not know what to make of meaning looks. 'We've got a new boy friend, have we?' was Mrs Boundy's next pleasantry. It was so patently absurd that Irene ignored it, though angry. She was amazed when Mrs Rawson began nodding and smiling at her and said, 'I think it's very romantic, my dear.'

Irene's wild hope of making a real friend of Mrs Rawson had long since bitten the dust. Mrs Rawson often chatted with her, but the conversation always ran along the same lines. Mrs Rawson would tell the same stories about her husband, always as if she had never told them before. Irene soon gave up making any but the most predictable contributions because otherwise she would have to repeat what she said any number of times. She had nevertheless become rather fond of the old lady and she was the more astonished that she should join in Mrs Boundy's stupid teasing. It occurred to her that perhaps Mrs Rawson thought they were talking about some programme they had been watching on telly, and she smiled back at her.

'Won't you tell us all about him, dearie?' said Mrs Boundy.

Finding everyone looking at her Irene said coldly, 'Who?'

'Oh, you can't keep it dark in a place like this. We know all about it,' said Mrs Boundy.

'Which is more than I do,' said Irene tartly.

'No need to be hoity-toity. We only want to be friendly,' said Mrs Boundy. 'But of course we all understand. Everyone is coy when it's an affair of the heart. Tell me, is he young?'

'Of course he's not young,' said somebody else.

'But middle-aged men can be very attractive. Mr Boundy wasn't exactly young when we first met. I was working in the Naafi then. We used to have some good times in those days, I'm telling you. Everybody in the kitchen had set their caps at him, but right from the start he had eyes only for me. I had a great way with the boys, you know. You can imagine there was a lot of jealousy . . .' Mrs Boundy had always rather talk about herself, to Irene's relief, because it meant that, apart from occasional references – 'I know just how you feel, dearie' – she lost sight of her original line of enquiry.

Irene was glad to get back to the safety of her own room, which she now shared only with Miss Benstead, as Birdie had gone home at the end of the previous week.

'My dear,' said Miss Benstead as soon as they were alone, 'that odious woman came in here this afternoon. I thought I should never get rid of her. Of course I knew nothing about it, but the rumour has got around that you have been visiting Mr Pollard. They've seen the bookrest and the chair and the gossips have invented the whole story on that basis.'

Irene hung her head. She could not let Miss Benstead believe a lie. 'I have met Mr Pollard,' she said. 'I have been over to visit him.'

'I see,' said Miss Benstead.

'But just because I've visited him and because he made the bookrest and the chair doesn't seem to me to be a very good reason for assuming we are having some sort of romance.'

'Their imaginations are starved,' said Miss Benstead. 'They have only to see a man out working in the fields and they start carrying on like a lot of stupid, giggling schoolgirls.'

That was only too true, Irene knew. Yet she felt humiliated by their suspicions. Couldn't she have a friend who was a man without that sort of talk? She took up a book, to read and forget all the unpleasantness. It was a book Harriet had lent her, because Ian had mentioned it. She was aware of him all the time as if he were watching her read and waiting for her opinion of the book, until she found she was not reading after all, but gazing out of the window. The sky was heavy and grey, fading imperceptibly into night. Not one figure passed along the lane. Why did she have to think everlastingly about Ian Pollard? At the now remote moment when Clare and Diana had been talking about a certain Hatty Moss, at least she had been free, at least she had been in control of the thoughts inside her own head. She could wish she had never met him.

After a while she noticed that Miss Benstead was not reading either. Their eyes met. 'I'm afraid this is prying, but does Sister know about your outings?' asked Miss Benstead.

'No,' said Irene.

'You must forgive me if I sound like an old schoolmistress,' said Miss Benstead. 'Sister is responsible for your well-being. If anything happened to you outside the hospital she might have to answer for it. I'm afraid she'll feel you've behaved badly to her.'

'Yes,' said Irene in a small voice. Miss Benstead had the habit of authority, even though the circumstances of their lives as fellow patients in Granstead Hospital gave her no power over Irene. 'What do you think I should do?' said Irene unhappily.

'Very likely Sister knows already, but if she doesn't it would be far better if you told her yourself, before the story leaks out in some other way, as it inevitably will.'

The idea that Sister might hear the gossip was very distasteful to Irene. Miss Benstead's advice seemed to be the only reasonable course to follow; she must get in first with her own version of the facts. She was a long time getting to sleep that night, her thoughts chasing round and round the same subjects. Sister's displeasure seemed to hang over her, suspended by a thread that a chance word might sever. She felt guilty for having deceived her. She phrased and rephrased her explanation. It would mean an end of all outings. Over and over again she persuaded herself that she did not want to see Ian Pollard any more.

But when morning came it turned out to be more difficult to make her confession than she had envisaged. Sister did not come her way. She asked Eileen to tell her she wished to speak to her, but Eileen exclaimed in astonishment, 'You don't want to tell Sister! Why should she find out?'

'Well, how has everyone else found out?' said Irene, a question she had not asked Eileen before as it sounded like an accusation.

'Somebody's seen you walking through Greenfields,' she said. 'The lady who brings round the telephone – she lives there. I daresay it was her, but it could easily have been somebody else. But nobody would say a word to Sister.'

Irene's guilt began to evaporate. 'You think it's all right, then?' she said.

'Look,' said Eileen, 'if Sister had found out, you'd know about it all right. If you ask me, I'd say don't go again, but as far as Sister's concerned, let sleeping dogs lie.'

Eileen seemed a bit offhand, less interested in the dilemma than Irene had expected. In truth, she was a bit miffed by Irene's secretiveness; also, although she had encouraged Irene to break bounds, she now saw it could lead to trouble. If Sister knew, even if Irene told her, she would be very angry and her displeasure would be felt by everyone in the ward. For general comfort she should not be told and the outings should be cut short.

The other patients continued to tease Irene about Ian Pollard, but Miss Benstead was very helpful and put a brake on the worst of the teasing by talking to her at table and in OT. Now at last Irene spoke to her of her resentment against occupational therapy. Ever since Birdie had told her Miss Benstead hated OT, Irene imagined they thought alike on this subject and her early desire to get to know Miss Benstead had been based on this assumption. But when she spoke with venom of being forced to spend her afternoons in such a pointless and degrading way, Miss Benstead was evidently surprised.

'But you see,' she said, 'if people were given the choice of going or staying in the ward, there are those who would stay just out of laziness – and those are the very people who get the most benefit from these activities. You and I may feel we have better things to do, but we go for the sake of other people. It's the same in a school – if the children were allowed to go only to those lessons they fancied, some would skip arithmetic and others would skip games. When they were older they would regret the mistake, but by then it would be too late to do anything about it.'

'But at least arithmetic is useful and games,' (Irene had hated games herself), 'games are good for the health.'

'Games teach us how to work as a team, one of the most important lessons in life.'

'But OT is quite useless, at least the way they do it here. We could be cooking, learning how to cope with life despite our disabilities. In real life you don't have to cope with making baskets and winding string round nails.'

'It may seem like a frill,' said Miss Benstead, 'but I believe it is one of the most worthwhile things they do here. Illness reduces people to helpless pawns, but in OT they have a chance to create something, to express themselves, and that can make them feel like human beings again.'

'Can you really call winding string round nails creating something and expressing yourself?' Irene asked in surprise.

'It may not be very satisfying to you or me, but just look how they enjoy themselves. It's the only time you see some of them absorbed. They lose the vacant expression they wear in front of the television.'

'But is it necessary to make quite such ugly, useless things?' objected Irene.

'Do you think they're ugly?' said Miss Benstead. 'I thought they were rather clever.'

Irene was nonplussed. Miss Benstead's tastes obviously differed from her own, not only in books but in everything else, and there is no arguing about taste. She remembered now she had rapped Harriet over the knuckles for making mock of the decor at Glebe Cottage. They like it like that, so what?

'Mrs Sparrow was very pleased with hers in the end,' said Miss Benstead. 'Mavis, from down the pool, was very taken with it, but Mrs Sparrow said, "I'm not giving it away. It's all my own work and I'm proud of it." '

Irene was taken aback once more, remembering how Birdie had said they could cut the string off and give it to someone else to do again. What would Birdie have said if Irene had admired the thing? Was it just her destructive attitude that made poor Birdie deplore what she was doing?

She remembered that Ian Pollard had criticized the way occupational therapy was done at Granstead so she quickly lumbered him with her own rejected point of view. Couldn't he understand that other people had needs and abilities different from his own? She started up a mental argument with him, making him say the most absurd things. She decided she was glad she would never have to see him again. For even if she didn't confess to Sister she had better follow Eileen's advice and put a stop to the outings. If Harriet came and they did not go out it would give the lie to all the odious gossip and teasing. And if she went out no longer there would be nothing to confess, nothing to feel guilty about.

Chapter XIV

HARRIET was not so easy to convince. 'Why can't you come?'
she exclaimed in disappointment. 'It's not going to rain.' The
weather had remained grey and heavy, but not a drop had
fallen.

'Let's go down into the garden. Then we can talk.' Miss
Benstead was deep in her book, but Irene felt she could not
talk freely in her presence. 'I don't think I should go out of
the grounds without Sister's permission,' she said when they
had got downstairs.

'But you did before. What's happened? This place isn't
a prison, you know,' said Harriet, using Ian Pollard's words.

Irene explained, but the explanation seemed very feeble.
Harriet laughed and laughed. 'To think it's me who's in love
with him!'

Harriet's laughter hurt, much to Irene's surprise. Why should
Harriet find romance for cripples quite so ridiculous? She
knew Harriet was laughing because the gossips were wrong in
this particular case, but she seemed to detect something beyond
that, and her bruised feelings contributed to her recapitulation
in a roundabout way. Harriet had arranged tea in the farmhouse garden as a special treat for herself, as Ian was invited
too and it would be just the three of them together, so much
better than a tête-à-tête, as, alone with him, Harriet would be
struck dumb. She needs me, thought Irene; even though I'm
crippled, I can talk to him and she can't.

Aloud she said, 'You know I only quarrel with him. But
if I'm so essential, all right, let's go this last time.' She had
quite decided she didn't want to go, but now she was glad to
be going.

Ian Pollard was walking on his crutches, a thing she had not seen him do before. He was taller than she expected. Sitting in the wheelchair he had appeared so thickset that she had imagined he would be stocky. 'Excuse me showing off,' he said. 'I am Mr Harris's prize patient, did you know? I was supposed never to walk again, but here I go.'

Irene watched him enviously. 'It'll be more difficult for me with the arthritis,' she said. 'He says he can't promise me anything.'

'But that's what I like about him,' said Ian Pollard. 'He's absolutely frank. The others all fob you off with false hopes. You know they're false, you know they know they're false, and they even know you know they know, but they still keep up the pretence.'

'Some people prefer it that way. They can't face the truth,' said Irene, immediately contrary. 'Mr Harris isn't popular with all the patients.'

'I don't believe that's true for you,' he said.

'But I'm not typical.'

'No one's typical.'

'Some people are more typical than others,' said Harriet laughing. It only seemed to amuse her to see them at cross purposes.

'You don't have to tell me people react differently,' he went on. 'Of course they do. Why, plenty of patients adore the very sort of OT you hate so much. It's their lifeline, and long may it continue so. But none of that makes any difference to the fact that I like plain speaking and so do you. Let me finish. It doesn't make any difference, either, to the fact that Mr Harris is a surgeon of genius, a master craftsman, and you ought to be jolly grateful you're on his list. I feel now that I owe it to him to stay alive, because he's put so much work into me. I'm his work of art, so I don't have any right to smash myself up again.'

'You did it on purpose, then,' said Irene.

'No, I didn't do it on purpose. I feel guilty enough when I see people like you waiting and waiting for the surgeon's knife, whilst there was I, whole in every limb, having a totally unnecessary accident and jumping the queue, wasting the surgeon's time. I hope I would never have risked other people's lives as well as my own, if I had tried to commit suicide. Nevertheless, I was pretty depressed at the time and the thought did pass through my head, as it was happening: does it matter if I never get home? Or rather, as there was no home waiting for me: does it matter if I come out of this alive?'

Irene felt angry with herself for having wasted so much time arguing with an imaginary villain, yet she couldn't quite rid herself of the rancour she felt against Ian Pollard. He had let her down by not being a villain. She was silent, and Harriet said, 'You mustn't think of killing yourself,' and then felt very foolish.

'It's all right – I don't want to die now,' he said. 'Quite apart from Mr Harris, I've lost the taste for it altogether. In fact I lost the taste for it immediately after the accident. I was trapped for several hours in the wreckage. Most of the time I was unconscious, but I remember lying with my head near a puddle. It was all amongst dead leaves and yet, at one place, through the dead leaves came some tiny threads of live grass. I remember it so very vividly and yet it was totally unreal to me – it had no connection with anything, no meaning whatsoever. Those threads of grass were a sort of abstract greenness. I could not understand what they were or what I was myself. Then I saw that they were grass and I was separate because I was alive and desperate to go on living.'

'Did you decide to live every moment of your life after that?' asked Irene.

'Yes,' he said, 'it was something like that story in *The Idiot*.' Harriet made a quick mental note of another book she had to read, but she pretended she knew just what they were talking about.

'And you didn't succeed,' said Irene.

'Of course not. Nobody does. That's the point of the story, isn't it?'

'Harriet told me that you never ate oranges because you

couldn't do anything else while you were eating an orange. Is that what you understand by living every minute? Because, if so, I think you've got the story all wrong.' Even while she spoke she wondered why she had to talk to him so defiantly.

He assumed a small penitent voice and said, 'Tell me what I ought to think.'

Ashamed of her aggressive attitude, she tried to speak more gently. 'Mavis told me that your trouble was that you weren't used to being ill. People tend to think that you miss out on everything by being crippled – and of course some people do. I don't *want* to be crippled, but it has given me some things I'm grateful for. I have to be passive. I have to sit still. My hands are too painful even to hold a book. But sometimes I see things that other people never see because they're too busy – very ordinary things, but perhaps I see them as intensely as your blades of grass. You don't have to be able to do some-thing else at the same time – that's a way of escaping from the present moment.'

'So you live every moment that you're in hospital?'

'No, of course not,' she said irritably. 'All the same, being in hospital forces me sometimes to live the odd moment in that way. The rest of the time is all wasted in pain and frus-tration and telly.'

'You see,' he said, 'I feel most alive when my mind's racing, when I'm working something out, when everything starts fitting together and the solution leapfrogs over all the difficulties that seemed to stand in its way. I know it's something different from what you're talking about – don't start ticking me off. I think I had a taste of the other in the crushed car, or else I might not even know what you mean. But I have my own kick and that's why I eat apples while I'm working and I can't spare the time to eat oranges.'

Harriet was delighted with the conversation. If only she could get Ian to talk like this. Timidly she asked, 'Can't you live both sorts of moments? I mean, the ones when you're working inventing something, and the others when you're not working, like now. I could even get you an orange.'

'No,' he said. 'As Irene says, you have to waste so much time in pain and frustration and television tracking down the few moments you really live. It's the pursuit of a lifetime, not something you do in off moments.'

Harriet had settled them in her favourite spot in the overgrown garden, close beside the summerhouse that was half collapsed under a load of honeysuckle. She went off to boil the kettle. When she was gone Ian Pollard said, 'She's a sweet child, really,' making Irene feel she was about a hundred. 'Somehow or other she doesn't give me the feeling that I'm an object of charity. That's one of the things I've hated most since my accident, being done good by. But you'll find fault with that.'

'You've got me all wrong,' said Irene. 'I don't like being done good by, either. It's just that nobody would accomplish anything if everybody was as afraid of their own motives as you are.' She was pleased to have at last produced an argument she had used so often against him in imagination. But of course his reply was different from any imagined reply he had given.

'It's not my motives I worry about, it's my ability to accomplish something actually useful. I'm an amateur playing about with high-flown ideas for wheelchairs which will never go into production. Sometimes I feel I ought to have stayed in hospital and I'd have learnt much more about what crippled people really need.'

Irene felt humbled. He was so much less short-sighted than the image she had made of him. 'What made you tell me about your accident?' she asked. 'Do you tell everyone?'

'No,' he said. 'Most people wouldn't understand what I was talking about.'

'What made you unhappy?' she asked. 'Why didn't you care if you died?' Harriet, who had come back with the tea, blenched; she would never have dared ask such a direct question.

Ian Pollard paused, as if weighing up possible answers. 'It seems,' he said, 'that I'm intolerable to live with in the long run. And that is a pretty depressing thought.'

Harriet was just working out what this meant in terms of her scant knowledge of his married life, when, to her horror, she heard Irene launch into the attack again.

'Both your wives left you? Or do you have more than two?'

Ian Pollard was taken aback. 'Who told you I had more than one?' he said.

'You said your *first* wife was called Eunice.'

'So I did.' He laughed shortly. 'We'll, since you are conducting this interrogation, no, I left Eunice. Margaret left me. Now are you satisfied? Let us eat our tea.'

Harriet was nervous lest he had been offended, but he seemed determined to make a success of the tea-party. He talked once more about the experimental kitchen. 'I should like to have a hand in a venture like that,' he said. 'I think I really could make a contribution because the situation would be designed to throw up the sort of problems I am good at solving. I could be a sort of consultant inventor. I feel frustrated now because I know people at Granstead could do with just that sort of help, but I'm not in a position to know what is needed and there's no point at all in solving imaginary problems.'

Irene spoke to him of Janice and some of the things that Janice found it difficult to do without help. She warmed to him that afternoon. If she had ever thought idly of friends she would have liked to have had, she would have imagined someone much more like herself, who shared her interests and shared her bent of mind. She wondered now how she could ever have found Ian Pollard like herself. He was a breath of fresh air to her with his positive practical drive and his outgoing warmth; it was such a relief to find someone who did not tie himself up in tight little knots, as she did herself.

Chapter XV

❦

No rain came and not a breath of air moved. In hospital Irene felt as if she could not breathe. The heavy atmosphere weighed on everyone like a threat, and it seemed to her that gossip hung like an unwholesome exhalation in the torpid air. On Wednesday there was a general reshuffle of beds to make room for new patients. Mrs Boundy and another old recidivist were moved into the small room with Miss Benstead and Irene.

Mrs Boundy was volubly indignant. How could anyone be expected to exist without television? It was a basic human right. Sister assured her it was only for a few days as the doctor would probably send her home. Mrs Boundy shut up very suddenly on hearing this and only opened her mouth again to complain that there was a draught from the window. It is always sufficient for one person to complain of a draught for every window to be hermetically sealed, whatever the other occupants of the room may think. Irene told herself that, since no air had been entering by the window, it could make no difference that it was shut; nevertheless the fetid atmosphere seemed to become yet more oppressive.

Irene gleaned one slight advantage from Mrs Boundy's presence. Since she had not confessed to Sister and no longer intended to confess to Sister, she felt guilty alone with Miss Benstead. Not that the latter made any reference to their conversation; it was just her presence that made Irene awkward.

On Thursday Mrs Boundy got her marching orders from Dr Roberts. She broke down in tears and desperately begged

him to let her stay longer. From pathos she progressed to accusation: what right had he to send her home without any
notice? Her house was empty, the bed had not been aired,
there was no food in the larder. How could she get someone
to come in and make ready for her before the weekend? It was
just because he had some other patient he wanted to move
into her bed.

Dr Roberts gave in. Sister was obviously furious. They were
always short staffed at the weekend and this particular weekend
there were more patients than usual. For the first time Irene
felt almost sorry for Mrs Boundy. If to be sent home was such
a blow to her, what could her life outside the hospital be like?
But her misery did not make her attractive. She became morose,
which had its advantages as she did not talk much, yet somehow she managed to exude injury and illwill.

That evening, after supper, Irene asked if she might stay a
little longer in the dayroom, to avoid the company in the ward.
To her surprise she found Janice had got herself wheeled over
to join her.

'Do you mind if I stay and keep you company?' asked
Janice.

'Of course not,' said Irene, though inwardly her heart sank.
Janice was sweet and kind, and she never meant to tell you
about her own troubles but, since her mind ran on them without
respite, when she spoke nothing else came to hand. Irene could
not bear the burden of Janice's tragedy. There was nothing she
could do to help, but since she had no practical or financial
problems herself she felt guilty. Perhaps this time she could
bring the conversation round to kitchen improvements and find
out something that would be useful to Ian Pollard. But first
she asked, 'How are the children?'

'I hope they're all right,' said Janice. 'They were so shy
when they came over here. It's not like them. I couldn't get a
word out of them.' Then she went on earnestly, 'You mustn't
think I regret having the children. It's not their fault – the
arthritis, I mean. Sometimes having a child can cure you of
it, you know. That might happen to you. It was just my luck

that it had to start that way. It's wonderful to have children. Ron adores them. I wouldn't want you not to have any children just because of me.'

This last surprised Irene. 'I wasn't thinking of having children,' she said.

'But you must,' said Janice. 'A marriage is never complete without children. I knew I had to tell you this. You must try and have children . . . even if it's very difficult. I mean, perhaps you should wait until after you've had your operation. But it's worth it – and there's always the chance that it might cure you. I just wanted to tell you I'm so happy for your sake. Ron is always so considerate. I hope you'll be as lucky as I've been. But a man likes that sort of thing sometimes . . .' Janice blushed and Irene realized for the first time that she was talking about sex: and Ian Pollard.

'You know,' said Irene gently, 'it's only a silly rumour Mrs Boundy started. There isn't any truth in it really. My friend Harriet takes me out in Mr Pollard's chair, that's all.'

Janice was not convinced. She smiled a very knowing smile. 'I hope it all works out for the best,' she said. 'I just felt I had to say that about . . . children. I know you won't take it the wrong way.'

Irene again tried to protest, but without making any impression. She no longer dared raise the subject of kitchen improvements as that would have meant talking about Mr Pollard. She could only allow Janice to talk on about the blessings of marriage, a subject which imperceptibly turned into Janice's present difficulties. 'But it won't be like that for you,' Janice added hastily without a trace of envy. 'It must be different for people with means.'

Irene was relieved when someone came to fetch them away. Presented to her with such well-meaning simplicity the whole idea of love and marriage amongst cripples became grotesque, almost obscene. How could 'means' make her wretched body fit for a marriage bed? How could anyone wish to marry her except for the most perverted motives? It was all right for Janice, married before she was ill; but for herself there could never be anything but the shadows of other people's lives watched in the magic mirror.

> *Or when the moon was overhead*
> *Came two young lovers lately wed . . .*

It might be bitter to have a life populated only by shadows, but any alternative was unthinkable.

Irene had seldom felt so miserable as she did after this kindly-meant advice from Janice. She had always known she was doomed to live an abnormal life but she had not constantly thought of the future in these terms — for how could anyone live from day to day in a constant knowledge of his own mischance? It had been her philosophy to live in the present; but the present in hospital was intolerable; she felt trapped, under constant pressure from gossip and teasing. There was no one she could talk to; she had lost contact with Miss Benstead, and anyway how could she talk to an old school-mistress about the things that were on her mind?

Even Eileen seemed to be avoiding her. She asked Linda, 'Is Eileen angry with me because I went out again?'

'You mustn't mind Eileen,' said Linda with a laugh. 'Terry's asked her to go out and she can't think of anything else.'

Irene felt first a jab of pain that Eileen, who had kept her informed of every stage of the drama, had failed to tell her of this triumph; and she realized that Eileen had not been telling her much these last few days and that she had not even noticed because she had been absorbed in her own affairs. But after that first hurt she felt the dull miserable pain of being alone in her plight; Eileen would be merry, in no mood to contemplate Irene's empty future; and anyway, what would Eileen think of it? Like Janice, would she think marriage was possible with sex thrown in as a kind of necessary torture or would she flinch away from the whole idea of love for cripples, preferring to ignore such problems? Irene remembered Harriet's laughter; she had meant nothing by it but it had hurt. She did not want Eileen to laugh like that at the gossip, nor did she want her to believe it . . .

Irene began to wonder whether perhaps the gossips were right and she was in love with Ian Pollard. She thought it over very coolly. She liked him despite being so much at odds with him – yes; and lately she had felt the warmth of friendship growing between them. Yet since that last meeting she no longer found herself thinking of him all the time – it had been her own hostility that obsessed her. The stupid gossip did not upset her because it was about him, but because it was a mockery of reality, of the stunted life she was doomed to lead. If only she could go out and talk seriously about these things with somebody from the outside world – or, more particularly, with Ian Pollard. He was wise and experienced; he would not try to comfort her with a happy future he did not believe in; but neither would he find the whole subject distasteful, better ignored.

But she could not hope to see him and talk to him again. She had told Harriet not to bring the wonderful chair. They had had their very last outing. On the way back to the hospital after the tea-party with Ian Pollard she had felt so happy that she had had no difficulty in sounding decisive and convincing Harriet; yet now she felt so desperate and claustrophobic that she longed to reverse that decision, and hoped that Harriet might just bring the chair after all.

She was disappointed. Harriet came without the chair. Mrs Boundy emerged from her all-engrossing misery at the sight of her. She hobbled over and caught her by the elbow – she had the habit of catching hold of people when she wanted to talk to them. 'How's our friend?' she asked in a penetrating whisper. She winked.

Harriet was too taken aback to say anything at all. The scared look she flung at Irene said, 'Is this woman in her right mind?'

'Mrs Boundy,' said Irene, 'nobody knows what you're talking about.'

Mrs Boundy began winking all the more strenuously. 'My young friend knows what we're talking about,' she said, tugging at Harriet's elbow. 'Don't you, dearie? Ain't you going to take Ireen out today to see you-know-who? She's been getting a real cross-patch lately and we can all guess why.'

'I'm afraid you're under some sort of a misunderstanding,' said Harriet. 'I've just come to visit Irene.'

'Don't think you can pull the wool over old Boundy's eyes!' said Mrs Boundy. 'She knows what you're up to all right.'

Harriet, whose arm had been released, bent over Irene and said, 'There are some of those hospital wheelchairs out in the corridor. Couldn't we go down in the garden?'

'Ask Sister if we can take one,' said Irene in a loud clear voice.

Harriet, who didn't know the difference between nurses and Sister, asked the first likely person she met. ' 'Course you can take one,' said Eileen. She wheeled it into the room. 'You're just going down into the garden, are you?' she asked.

'Yes,' said Irene firmly. 'We just want to go out into the garden.'

'Don't think I don't know where the two of you's off to,' cackled Mrs Boundy.

'We're going down into the garden,' said Irene coldly, 'so that we can talk together in peace.'

'So he's down in the garden, is he? Give him my love,' was Mrs Boundy's parting shot.

'She must be off her head,' said Harriet in the lift.

'She's miserable at the moment,' said Irene. 'That makes her worse than usual.'

Harriet had not planned every move, but she had done certain things 'in case'. For instance, she had brought the wonderful chair round as far as her own house. 'If she wants to go out after all,' she had said to herself, 'then we can change chairs before we get to the unmade road.' What went on inside the hospital was unreal to her. She did not believe in Sister's authority, and as for the gossip, that was absurd.

For Irene what went on inside the hospital was too real. She was desperate to escape from it even temporarily, whatever the consequences might be. She felt guilty about Eileen. She would not have lied to her if she had known what they were going to do. But their friendship, if you could call it that, had grown cold. 'She doesn't understand,' said Irene to herself as she treacherously acquiesced to Harriet's plan.

Chapter XVI

HARRIET hated finding intruders who had wandered down the lane or into the farmyard at the Glebe. She might adapt to passers by elsewhere along the green lanes, but this was holy ground. Someone had driven an ancient Morris Minor right into the farmyard and had chosen this particular spot to jack it up and disembowel it. A pair of legs protruded from underneath. What cheek, thought Harriet and took no notice when a head came out to peer at them. They passed by and went on to the back door of the farmhouse.

Harriet had already pushed Irene over the sill before she realized there was a strange woman sitting on the settle. Ian Pollard had his back to them. He was sitting at the table, right across the room from his guest. As they entered he was speaking.

'You always were good at heaping on coals of fire, Eunice,' he said bitterly.

The woman sitting on the settle was crying. Tears ran down her cheeks and she did not bother to wipe them away.

At that moment the youth from under the car appeared behind them. 'I say, Dad,' he said ' – you don't happen to have any spanners do you?'

Ian Pollard turned and saw them. 'Show him the things in the workshop, Harriet,' he said. 'There's a good girl.'

They were glad to extricate themselves from an awkward situation. The youth was tall like his father and seemed to be in good spirits, untouched by the troubles of his elders. As soon as he was inside the workshop he forgot about spanners. 'I say, what a place!' he exclaimed. 'Was this here already or did he have it all fixed up for himself?'

'He had the workbench built,' said Harriet. Her voice sounded surly. Leaving Irene in the gully where the chair stood level, she had gone over to the workbench and opened a drawer where tools were kept. But the lad was far more interested in the diagrams and drawings and small models which had been left lying on the bench.

'What's he been up to?' he said, eagerly turning over sheets of calculations. 'By the way, I'm his son Jerry. He won't mind if I look at these things. What's your name?' But without waiting for an answer he picked up a model of the sprung wheel and exclaimed, 'What's this?'

He must have seen the wheels on the wheelchair earlier without noticing them particularly, because at this point he turned and flung himself on his hands and knees and began to examine them. 'Do you mind?' he said cheerfully to Irene and pushed the chair up and down, still kneeling beside it. She showed him how to release the brake. Harriet stood by the workbench biting her lip. There was a sulky closed expression on her face and Irene could not guess what she was thinking.

They were interrupted by the appearance of his mother. She was blowing her nose and stumbled against the threshold and then stood there uncertainly, obviously blinded by tears. 'Jerry?' she said.

'Mum?'

'We must go.'

'For Chrissake! I thought we'd stay here at least all afternoon. I can't make out why it's boiling. I'm just trying to dismantle the pump. Wait a minute.' He strode past her and disappeared into the farmhouse. She stood leaning against the door jamb, blowing her nose. Harriet and Irene pretended they weren't there.

Presently Jerry reappeared. 'Look Mother,' he said, 'you'd better go for a nice country walk or something. It'll take me at least an hour to see to the motor. I know you don't understand these things but I honestly can't drive off as it is.' He put his arm round her and she began to sob on his shoulder.

'There, there, Mumsie,' he murmured. 'Everything's going to be all right.'

When her sobs subsided she asked if there was anywhere where she could wash her face. Harriet, who was still standing by the workbench biting her lip, suddenly came to life. 'I'll show you,' she said.

From where she sat Irene could see through the door of the workshop to the kitchen door of the house. She saw Harriet take Mrs Pollard not to the kitchen door but round the corner of the house. A moment later she reappeared and herself went through the kitchen, presumably to open the front door from the inside. Jerry had not moved.

'All coasts clear, do you think?' he asked when a minute had elapsed after Harriet's last disappearance. 'Well, here goes.' He crossed to the kitchen door and went in. Presently he reappeared, wheeling his father. Ian Pollard looked drawn and tired. He gave Irene a sad smile. It was a smile of complicity, as if he expected her to understand, and in that moment Irene knew that, whatever sympathy might be due to the unknown wife, all hers went to him.

He began to explain about the wheels. At first he sounded weary and preoccupied, but it was a subject on which he could wax enthusiastic even when his audience was quite incapable of understanding about pistons or castors, and this time he had someone who could ask intelligent questions. The son obviously took after the father in more than looks. It appeared that he was already reading engineering at Cambridge. Irene found pleasure in watching the two of them together, although their conversation was far beyond her comprehension. Jerry had suggestions of his own to make, one of which hadn't even occurred to his father. A new factor had entered his calculations and his mind was racing. Perhaps this was one of the moments when he really lived: Irene had never seen him so alert and concentrated.

They had moved over to the drawing board, leaving her abandoned in the centre of the room. 'Do you mind us treating you like something in a test tube?' said the boy. Irene had liked him from the moment he had knelt down by the wheelchair and said 'Do you mind?', treating her as a human being in full possession of her faculties.

'I only hope I'm not in your way,' she said.

Jerry's suggestion proved abortive, but it took some time for his father to demolish it. The exercise was clearly exhilarating and his face was alight at the end of it, all else forgotten. But then he looked at his watch and became sombre.

'I suppose Harriet is looking after your mother,' he said. 'You had better see to that motor of yours.'

'Don't you think we could stay here after all?' said Jerry. 'You must have stacks of rooms upstairs. Or, if you don't want us in the house, we could find some hotel in the town.'

His father was silent.

'Mum was so keen to come. She's been on at me for weeks that I ought to come over and see you. Then, when at last I said I would, she said, as if it was all a new idea that had suddenly occurred to her, why didn't I take her along and we could spend the weekend somewhere on the coast. But I guessed what she was plotting all the time.'

'It's very touching that you should want to play this fairytale part, reuniting your parents,' said Ian Pollard, speaking with difficulty as if he had to drag the words out of himself. 'But it isn't as easy as all that. I know I haven't got a leg to stand on – sorry, I didn't mean to make a pun.' He paused, covering his eyes with his hand. 'Irene will understand what I mean. I know your mother wants to forgive all. She wants to be a saint, to sacrifice herself, to devote herself to looking after me. But I'm afraid I can't consent to be the occasion of her sacrifice. That sort of thing is more blessed to give than to receive, if the devil may quote scripture.'

Jerry gave a sigh and began to turn over the papers that lay on the bench. 'You've been working on several different projects,' he said.

'The drawer where the spanners are is already open,' said his father.

Ian Pollard remained sitting in the workshop with the drawing board in front of him, doing nothing. The light that had lately shone in his face had gone out, and he looked defeated and miserable. A long time elapsed before he remembered Irene again. 'I'm sorry,' he said. 'This must be an awful bore for you.'

'Don't worry about me,' said Irene. 'I'm used to getting left around. I'm sorry I'm in your way.'

'In my way?' he said. 'I'm glad to have you here. You're the only sane person in this outfit.'

After another long lapse of time he said, 'Here they come at last.' A look of pain had passed over his face. Through the window Irene caught sight of Harriet and his wife. Jerry was speaking to them; then they disappeared from view. A few minutes later Harriet appeared at the workshop door. She did not look at nor speak to Ian.

'It's going to rain,' she said to Irene. 'I felt the first drops. I'd better take you back.'

It was late anyway and they had the extra trouble of changing chairs on the way. The sky had become darker and lower. Harriet seemed preoccupied with getting her back before the heavens opened. She said little on the way back and it was only as they were approaching the hospital that Irene said, 'It was kind of you to look after Mrs Pollard like that.'

'I don't know why you say that,' said Harriet. 'I like her.'

The defensive tone struck Irene and she did not quite understand the meaning of it.

Chapter XVII

THE rain when it fell was a sudden deluge and although they only had fifty yards to go Irene was soaked to the skin. Eileen met them with a bitter reproach: 'You *said* you was only going in the garden.'

'We only *meant* to go in the garden,' said Irene. 'And then we changed our minds.'

'We can't just stand here talking,' said Eileen. 'I'd better get you out of those wet things. Luckily for you Sister ain't around.'

Harriet longed to be helpful but she didn't know what to do and Eileen ignored her efforts almost rudely. 'You'd better be going,' she told her, 'or Sister'll come back and smell a rat.'

'I really didn't plan it. I wouldn't have told you a lie,' said Irene.

'That don't make much difference now, do it?' said Eileen who was being just a trifle rough in pulling off the wet clothes. 'The sooner we get you out of these things the better.'

Harriet had departed and Irene's clothes had been changed before Sister appeared in the doorway. Eileen was just rubbing Irene's head with a towel.

'When you have finished drying Miss Paxton's hair, nurse, bring her along to my room,' said Sister. 'I want to have a word with her.' Her voice was icy. She evidently knew already.

When she had gone Eileen said, 'There you are. Now we'll all have to face the music.'

'But I'll tell her you had nothing to do with it, that you didn't even know I was going.'

Eileen softened a little. 'Keep your chin up,' she said. 'It's not the end of the world.' She pushed Irene down the corridor and knocked at Sister's door. 'I'll keep my fingers crossed,' she said.

Sister did not even look at Irene to begin with. She was busy with something else. At last she said grimly, 'I gather this is not the first time you have left the hospital grounds to visit Mr Pollard at Glebe Farm. Is that so?'

'Yes. At least, we didn't always go to visit Mr Pollard but we have been outside the hospital grounds on several occasions.'

'We?' said Sister. 'Who is we?'

'My friend Harriet and I. Nobody else had anything to do with it. I want to make that clear — it is entirely my own responsibility.'

'You think none of the nurses knew you were leaving the grounds?' asked Sister sarcastically. 'You think that sort of thing does not get about in a place as small as this?'

'When they found out they told me not to do it again. But I ignored that and went again. It is entirely my own fault.'

'So they knew you had gone and they did not think fit to inform me. Tell me, was Nurse Poolley one of those who "told you not to do it again"?'

'I think most people in the ward knew about it, Sister,' said Irene trying to shield Eileen. 'I told Nurse Poolley that I was only going down into the garden this afternoon.'

'I see,' said Sister. There then elapsed a long silence during which Sister searched in a cupboard for something. At last she shut the cupboard door and sat down behind her desk and gave her whole attention to Irene.

'I hope you realize, Ireen, that everyone in this hospital is doing everything within their power to help you to get better; that all of us here are concerned not only for your health but for your happiness; that we all realize that what you have to bear because of your illness is very hard for you, possibly harder for you, because you are young, than it is for those who have not been stricken until late in life. We know this and we are sorry for you and we would like to do what is possible to alleviate your condition. But knowing this I would also add that you do not do much to help yourself and you take precious little thought for the other patients in this ward.'

Irene had not expected an attack like this and she did not understand what Sister meant. 'What thought should I have taken?' she asked.

'You must be aware that in a place like this where a number of people are shut up together week after week, all of whom have plenty of reason to be depressed, it is very easy for everyone to be miserable. It only takes one person who openly indulges in gloom and despondency – the mood soon communicates itself to everyone else. Most people realize this and they do their best to be cheerful for the sake of other people. I am in charge of this ward and I am concerned not only for the physical welfare of all the patients, but also for what I can only call their psychological welfare, because I know that no treatment however modern, however scientific, can achieve maximum results if the patient has been demoralized, has lost hope or is just in very low spirits. Now I know you are young and there is not much company for you in a ward where most people, with the exception of Janice, are over sixty; nevertheless I feel you could have made more effort to be sociable. You think it's so superior not to watch television, but wouldn't it have been better to have pretended to take some interest? You thought you were made of finer metal, you held yourself aloof, you thought nobody suffered as you did. But let me tell you, Ireen, the best people are those who forget themselves, forget how superior they are, and do what they can to help other people.'

Sister's harangue was not without its effect on Irene. She saw all her past behaviour in another light. She had tried – just a little bit. She had talked to herself about accepting the hospital. But she had never thought about the depressing effect she might have on the other patients; she was carried away by the force of Sister's eloquence and for the time being it all seemed true and convincing.

'I could see you were unhappy in the ward,' Sister went on, 'and I thought it would be better, both for you and for the others, if I moved you into one of the smaller rooms. I asked Mrs Sparrow if she would mind going in there with you, because I noticed she was one of the few people you deigned to speak to. It seemed to work out well. You looked more cheerful. You seemed to get on with Miss Benstead too. But apparently you were still dissatisfied. You still indulged in this childish self-centred illusion that the world was against you, that everything in the hospital was devised only out of spite against you. Do you know why patients are not allowed to leave the grounds?'

'It's something to do with insurance.'

'You see, you already know that there is a good reason for this rule. It's not just something that I, individually, have made up out of spite.' Sister then went on at great length about responsibility. She enlarged upon what accidents might have happened and she made a great drama about getting wet and what disastrous effects it might have on someone in Irene's condition. Irene knew that a cold could cause her a lot of pain, but as it happened her clothes had been changed so quickly that she could scarcely be in more danger than she was daily from going in the pool. However, she knew she was in the wrong and this sort of risk was a real one: if she got a cold in hospital she would not be able to continue with treatment; also, she might pass it on to others. But Sister was becoming very tedious and Irene found it difficult to feel suitably guilty. Sister was now arguing that because some patients had to be confined to the hospital – surgical cases and so on – therefore all the patients must resign themselves to the same limitations "for the sake of others". She had succeeded, though perhaps she was not aware of it, in making Irene feel rotten and selfish a few minutes earlier but this time Irene only felt rebellious. She found herself wondering what Ian would think of Sister's reasoning. The thought of him suddenly reminded her of the situation at the Glebe that afternoon which had been swept right out of her mind by the events on her return to the hospital; once reminded of it she could think of nothing else. Her thoughts ran over what had happened and what had been said, exploring and re-exploring everything that had taken place.

Irene had hardly been listening to the long tirade when suddenly a sentence caught her ear which brought her own stream of thought to an abrupt halt. 'What am I going to say to your mother when she discovers that you have been paying secret visits to a divorcee?' Irene felt her heartbeat race; her indignation was such that for the moment she could not speak.

'Whilst you have been entrusted to my care,' Sister went on dramatically, 'you have been having clandestine meetings with a man of what I can only call doubtful morals. Can you imagine how I feel? I know you are legally of age now, but I have known you since you were a child and I still think of you as a child who has been entrusted to my care by her loving parents. When your mother left I assured her – what reason had I to do otherwise? – that she need have no worries about you whilst you were in Granstead. Little did I dream that you would go behind my back to pay these secret visits to a strange man . . .'

This is nothing but mocked-up melodrama, thought Irene furiously – Sister doesn't believe a word of it.

' . . . How can I answer for what went on at these clandestine assignations?'

At last Irene broke in, her voice sounding unnaturally shrill – 'Before you let your imagination run riot, let me remind you that with my hips I am physically incapable of the act of copulation.' She was so furious that she chose the crudest words she could think of.

Sister blushed. She went absolutely scarlet.

My word, she'll hate me, thought Irene. But at that moment it was a triumph.

Later it no longer seemed such a triumph. She thought of the two hip operations and the long spells she would have to spend in this same hospital after them. She thought of that blush. Could Sister ever forgive her for such a show-down?

She was taken from Sister's office into the dayroom where they had started their supper. They were in the midst of a conversation and fell silent on her entry, so she knew they had been talking about her.

'No more outings to see your boyfriend now,' said Mrs Boundy, almost with glee.

'Never you mind what Sister says,' whispered her neighbour. 'Once you go out of this place she can't do a thing to you.'

'No more outings anyway, dearie,' said another. 'Just look at the weather.'

'Perhaps *he*'ll come to see you.'

'He won't be able to go out in the rain neither.'

'He comes to the pool, don't he?'

'The weather's broken for good. It'll be winter now before we know where we are.'

The rain was falling torrentially outside. There were no curtains in the dayroom and they could not shut out the lightning. Every now and again the electric lights faltered and for a moment everyone was silent waiting for darkness. The thunder fell right overhead. Then someone would laugh and everyone would start talking at once.

After supper Mrs Boundy and their other room-mate went to watch television and Irene was alone with Miss Benstead. The storm had moved on, but the rain was still falling heavily, drumming on the corrugated iron roofs of the bicycle sheds below the windows. Miss Benstead was reading imperturbably. Irene had a book in her hands but she was not reading. The noise of the rain seemed interminable, unvarying, drumming inside her head. She could not escape from it. She could not escape from the hospital. She could not escape from the nightmare in which she was caught. She was still haunted by Sister's earlier reproaches. She had been unsociable, superior, she had not thought how her own misery might affect others. But hadn't she tried a bit? Hadn't she been friendly with Mrs

Rawson, with Janice, and of course with Birdie and Miss Benstead? Could she be expected to be sociable with all of them? It was so difficult to think of things to say. It had been the same this suppertime. Some of them had meant to be kind, but how could she be other than chilly when they insisted on insulting her with this absurd humiliating talk of Mr Pollard? And that brought back Sister's horrible insinuations, all that about having clandestine assignations with a divorcee. What did she really know about his morals? Irene was crying with rage and indignation that Sister could say such insulting things to a helpless cripple who for the time being was totally within her power. For surely she could not believe the gossip? Or did everybody really believe in this absurd romance? After all, she would never have accused Janice of bad faith.

Suddenly she could bear the tension no longer. 'Miss Benstead, do *you* believe the stories about me and Mr Pollard?' she asked in a strangled voice.

Miss Benstead looked up from her book, moving her reading glasses down her nose. 'My dear,' she said, 'there is no need to upset yourself about what that stupid woman says.'

'Thank you,' said Irene. 'I'm glad someone doesn't believe it. Because Sister does.'

Miss Benstead removed her glasses. 'I guessed something had happened,' she said.

Irene told her story. 'I know I shouldn't have gone out without her permission. I know I should have told her long ago.'

'She had no right to speak to you like that,' said Miss Benstead decisively. 'I would not have credited Sister with such vulgarity.'

'I was very rude to her,' said Irene. 'I lost my temper.' She did not confess the 'vulgar' form her rudeness had taken.

'It is always a mistake to lose one's temper,' said Miss Benstead, 'however much one may have been provoked.'

'I know,' said Irene. 'I don't think she'll ever forgive me for the things I said.'

'Come, come. She'll have second thoughts. She must realize she's made rather a fool of herself.'

That's why she won't forgive me, thought Irene, remembering that blush. It occurred to her then that Sister might write to her mother; the dreadful drama would not be confined to the hospital. Luckily any letter sent to Italy was likely to miss her mother. But suppose such a letter awaited her on her arrival home? Perhaps she had better write a letter herself to explain things differently. But if Sister didn't write she didn't want to 'explain' things at all. She had already written to tell her mother about the chair and their walks in the country. Perhaps she should just write and say Sister was very angry because she had gone out without permission. She would not mention the stories about Mr Pollard unless – but then Sister would be sure to buttonhole her mother when she came to visit her. Whatever would her mother make of it? She wouldn't believe it – no – but she'd get hold of some wrong end of the stick.

That weekend seemed to go on for ever. The nurses were all a bit subdued. Sister's displeasure had fallen on all of them equally. Eileen was relieved that there was nothing special for her. She had forgiven Irene entirely – it was not her nature to bear grudges and seeing how miserable Irene looked had quite melted her heart.

'It won't go on for ever,' she assured her. 'Anyway, you're going out this week, aren't you? Once you're out of this place who cares what Sister thinks?'

Irene asked her about Terry. Eileen's eyes sparkled as she told her about their date and how it had all come about. 'But I mustn't stand here chatting. Sister's on the warpath. Nobody can do a thing right and I guess she'll be mad if she finds me talking to you when somebody else is crying out for me.'

Irene never asked Eileen what she thought of the gossip; she avoided the subject. Somehow it had got round the ward that Mr Pollard was married. The other patients infuriated Irene by telling her consolingly that all men were a bad lot.

Miss Benstead proved a tower of strength; she would interrupt such consolations with, 'Nonsense! I've known many excellent men in my time,' resolutely refusing to understand what they were driving at. This even afforded Irene some amusement, to see the old gossips discomforted, trying to make themselves plain without speaking openly, for they were all a bit in awe of Miss Benstead.

Irene never knew that Harriet came to see her but was waylaid by Sister and told that she was too tired to receive visitors. Nor did she know that Harriet's mother rang up to find out what was wrong with her. She lived in a vacuum, cut off entirely from the world beyond the ward. At the weekend they never left the ward at all. Through the window she could see that other world, all washed and fresh and looking curiously close at hand after the rain; it was so clear that you could have almost touched it, leaning out of the window, and yet in fact it was further away than it ever had been. It was strange to see the tiny figure, that was undoubtedly Harriet, stand, shading her eyes against the sun, gazing across at the hospital. She could no more hope to catch her attention than to catch that of actors on the television screen.

She longed for Monday when they would go down to the pool and she could speak to Mavis and establish some kind of communication with the outside world. But when she awoke on Monday morning she realized her period had started and she would not be able to go down to the pool. Her last week in hospital would be without purpose, and she could not hope to go home till she had seen Dr Roberts on Thursday. When she thought of going home she had to remind herself that it would be an escape from this present hell, for she felt a numb regret at the prospect of leaving Granstead without seeing Ian Pollard again. And Harriet, of course. But, she thought wryly, the gossips would be confirmed in their suspicions if they knew how much I think of him. But that was what made it so bitter! If Ian Pollard had meant nothing to her it would not have mattered how much they had twisted the story – she could have ignored it, however distasteful it was to her. But they were trampling on real feelings, they were defiling something that was precious to her in a way their 'vulgar' minds could never appreciate. Wasn't it only natural that she should want to know how he fared after that fateful afternoon? She could write to him, but she would rather have known something of what he felt first, rather than writing in the dark.

It was when she thought of a letter that she had a premonition of what the full effect of Sister's scandal-mongering might be. What would her mother think? She had to depend on someone else in everything, even to post letters. It was not so much that she feared an absolute prohibition, as that she dreaded the ordeal of endless explanations. 'It would be better if you didn't write,' her mother would say. 'I know Sister is exaggerating and you're not in love with him, but for that very reason it isn't necessary to write and I really think it would be better if you didn't.' She could hear the arguments going on and on and the more she insisted on writing the more would her mother believe it was unwise. Of course she could write a letter secretly, covering it up every time her mother came into the room, and get someone else to post it on the quiet. But her friendship with Ian Pollard was something healthy and happy and open and innocent. Why should she be forced to make it a sinister clandestine affair?

She was pursuing these thoughts on Monday evening. There was a visiting hour in the evening and she had hoped that Harriet might come after all, though she had begun to suspect that Sister had put a stop to her visits. The first visitors arrived and there was no one for her. So as not to remain in suspense, watching the door all hour long, she gazed out of the window at the familiar, much loved scene. Suddenly she was surprised by a familiar voice.

'But who hath seen her wave her hand
Or at the casement seen her stand . . .'

'Uncle William!' she exclaimed. 'I thought you were in Turkey.'

'I got back yesterday,' he said, 'and hurried over here to

134

make my offering of Turkish delight. Tomorrow I have to go to London Airport to meet your mother and we shan't be back in time to visit you, so I decided I must slip over this evening.' He unwrapped his parcels before he asked, 'Well, my Lady of Shalott, what's this I hear?

A bowshot from her bower eaves
He rode between the barley-sheaves . . .'

'Sister told you?' said Irene.

'Yes, that admirable lady waylaid me on the stairs and we had a long consultation – otherwise I would have been with you earlier. I've promised to thrash the whole matter out.'

Irene realized with relief that it would be infinitely easier to explain things to her uncle than to her mother. He would see the absurdity of the situation. He would not be affronted on her behalf, he would just be amused. And there would be no danger of his suspecting that her feelings were more involved than she cared to confess, which is something all mothers are prone to suspect. Finally, he would be able to handle both Sister and her mother.

When she had told her tale he said, 'What I'll do is, I'll go over this very evening and make the acquaintance of this gentleman and decide if he's the sort of person I can allow my niece to know. Then I'll nip back and fix it up with Sister. Never fear, that woman shall be as wax in my hands.'

That evening, long after visitors had been turned out, he stuck his head round the door and made the victory sign. 'Your friend Harriet will call for you tomorrow,' he said, and was gone.

Miss Benstead gave her one last bit of sound advice. 'You'd better apologize to Sister now, and let bygones be bygones.'

'Yes,' said Irene and this time she made no delay in following the advice.

Sister was gracious and condescending and explained rather stiffly why the insuperable rule could be waived. 'Your uncle is your next of kin for the time being, until your mother arrives home,' she said and Irene did not ask 'What about my father?'

She rather doubted anyway that the next-of-kin thing had any place in the rule book.

'It is very kind of you,' she said. 'I hope no one else will think that it's unfair.'

Then Sister delivered her last bombshell. 'As Mrs Pollard has come to look after her husband, there can be no impropriety in your visiting them.'

Chapter XVIII

HARRIET came to fetch her as arranged. With full authorization they were even able to leave by the back door, by way of the bicycle sheds and coal bunkers. Harriet had said nothing about the happenings at the Glebe so far. When they were out in the open Irene asked, 'So they stayed after all?'

'Jerry never fixed the car. I can't get him to tell me whether he did it on purpose.' Harriet spoke slowly. She did not seem eager to tell the whole story.

'Please put me in the picture,' said Irene.

Harriet laughed. 'Do you remember how you said the Glebe was like a picture to you and you expected to come up against the canvas round every corner? How shall I put you in the picture? Paint in an extra little figure?'

Why is she being so obstructive, thought Irene. 'No,' she said aloud, 'I want you to paint the rest of the picture round about me. I want to know what's happened.'

'Eunice stayed with us at first, but she's moved into the farmhouse now. They've borrowed beds from us. Jerry insists on sleeping in the "haunted" room – though of course it isn't really haunted. We had a great drama because the kitchen flooded with all that rain and Mavis was quite sure it was the water bed that had burst.' She laughed.

But what Irene wanted to know about was the feelings of the people concerned. Ian's feelings, Harriet's feelings. What did it matter which room Jerry slept in or what Mavis thought about the water bed? 'Has she come back for good?' she asked.

'He left her, you know,' said Harriet sharply. 'You can't really talk about her "coming back".'

'What makes you so prickly?' said Irene. 'I've been cut off

in that wretched hospital and I only want to know what's happened. There was a time when you could talk of nothing else but Ian Pollard.'

'All right. She and Jerry are staying here till term starts, but what will happen after that I don't know. Jerry goes back to Cambridge in the first week in October.' Then she went on with much greater animation, 'My parents have decided to send me to a cramming establishment just outside Cambridge. It's going to be rather jolly. Jerry'll be in his second year at Trinity.'

Irene tried a shot in the dark. 'Have you fallen in love again?'

There was a pause. Irene could not see Harriet's face. 'I don't know. It's different,' she said at last, and then added more briskly, 'I've quite got over that stupid crush.'

What is she really thinking or feeling? thought Irene. 'Was it so stupid?' she asked. 'I believe it did great things for you. Why should you discount it altogether, just because it wasn't reciprocated, which in the circumstances was surely a good thing?' Then suddenly she guessed – 'Do you feel guilty now that his wife's come back? All right, not "come back", but tell me what words I ought to use. I believe it's just because you feel you've wronged her that you're so defensive on her behalf. You've got to take her side to make up for having been in love with him.'

Harriet digested this, but said at last, 'Anyone would take her side. Wait till you meet her. She's awfully nice.'

'And Ian?' asked Irene. 'How does he take it all?'

'He's absolutely foul to her!' said Harriet with feeling. 'He snaps at her the whole time. I don't know how she puts up with it. She must be a saint.'

Irene decided she didn't like saints. She asked no more questions. Eunice met them in the farmyard. She came running in her eagerness.

'I've been longing to meet you,' she began. 'You really must forgive me – I hardly noiced anyone the other day. But now I've heard so much about you! and we've all been so worried because they told us you were ill. I thought perhaps you got soaked going back to the hospital in that downpour. It was terrible wasn't it?' She gave Irene no time to reply, but swept on, 'Ian talks so much about you. I've been so much looking forward to meeting you. We had hoped you might have come earlier. We were so delighted when your uncle came round last night. Such a charming man! Ian was so pleased to meet him. I would have asked him to stay to supper, but Harriet's parents had kindly asked us to go round there. I hope he wasn't offended, but I haven't really mastered the Aga yet and the whole place had been flooded, did Harriet tell you? . . .'

There seemed to be no way of halting the nervous spate of words. Poor Ian, thought Irene. I don't wonder if she gets on his nerves. It was some time before Harriet managed to ask, 'Is Jerry in the workshop with his father?'

'They're both in there. Will you take her?' said Eunice.

'You take her,' said Harriet.

'I think it would be better if you did,' said Eunice. 'You know about the chair.'

But Harriet was equally unwilling to go into his presence. 'The chair's easy,' she said. 'Just try it.'

'He doesn't like being interrupted,' said Eunice.

'Then let's not interrupt him,' said Irene.

'But he wants to see you,' said Eunice.

Irene wished she could get up and walk in, but she was at the mercy of other people's contradictions.

'I'll take you,' said Eunice at last. 'He did say he wanted to see you.' No sooner had she opened the door than she began apologizing for the interruption.

'It's quite all right, Eunice. There's no need to apologize,' he said. The edginess showed in his voice. 'You'll have to put that chair at the bottom of the gully or she'll be sitting crooked.'

Eunice couldn't see what was required and burst into yet more nervous apologies.

'Jerry, do it for her,' he said.

139

'I always do everything wrong,' she wailed.

'You don't do everything wrong,' he corrected her testily. 'It's the first time you've brought that chair in here. We'll take a break, Jerry. I want to have a chat with Irene. Your uncle tells me you go home at the end of the week, so it's probably the last chance we'll have of seeing one another.'

The others retired. He watched them go and then sighed. 'You see I'm behaving very badly,' he said meekly.

She smiled at him. 'Not really,' she said.

'Aren't you going to tick me off? You always used to tick me off. Tell me, why do we behave like this? I'm in the wrong and yet it's she who's so nervous of giving offence. She's tremendously happy and yet all I do is snap at her.'

'Isn't that the way people behave? Why ask me? I'm only young and I have no experience of life.'

'Somehow you don't seem young, not in many ways. Illness has set you apart from the hurly-burly. You called yourself an observer. Harriet never observes, nor Jerry, because they're in the thick of it all – they can only feel their own feelings. I think of you sitting up there at the hospital window, seeing us all very small, in perspective.'

'My uncle compared me to the Lady of Shalott. I do feel cut off from life like her. I am half sick of shadows, she said, and so am I. I want to be part of the hurly-burly. I don't feel so very wise.'

'Everyone feels they're missing out on life from time to time,' he said gently. 'I'm sorry. I shouldn't have put it like that. All I mean is that I can talk to you and have some hope of being understood. Harriet and Jerry, poor babes, they're so naïve and everything's so simple for them. They landed me in this mess, you realize. Jerry and that blasted car of his. If I had had the use of my legs I'd have got it on the road in no time – and so could he, but by that time he'd set his eyes on Harriet. That was one reason. Also he'd taken it into his head that Mum and Dad ought to get together again. Harriet, the sweet child, had also decided that a happy ending was in order, so she's been aiding and abetting him all along. Even the weather stuck an oar in – the rains came, the floods rose and no one would leave me to cope by myself. Dear old Mavis decided "it was meant" and like everyone else she's benignly hoping that we'll live happily ever after.' He came to a stop. 'I must sound very sour,' he added.

'You're not happy in any way? Not to have Jerry working with you?'

There was a long silence. 'To tell you the truth I'm happy to have Eunice here. Don't judge her too harshly – you must remember that I'm fond of her. She's nervous at the moment and that makes her gush, which I can't stand, and apologize compulsively the whole time. In fact she's driving me half out of my mind at the moment.' He shook his head with a sad defeated look. 'Well, anyway, I'm thankful it makes me respectable in Sister's eyes. Better not tell her it's my first wife.'

'You talk about me seeing things in perspective,' said Irene bitterly. 'You don't know what it's like being shut up in there. I lose all sense of proportion. Everyone does. I daresay Sister half believed all she said. She may even have believed it all. Perhaps it's not like this in the men's wards, but when women are shut up together . . . I don't know how to explain it. In some people it brings out the petty tyrant and the others just have to invent some drama, some romance, some stupid bit of semi-obscene gossip. What's so humiliating is that it was so stupid, it was unreal, but at the time life seemed totally unbearable. I'd even have given up the operations so as not to go in there again under Sister, just because I'd said something to make her blush and I thought she'd never forgive me.'

'You get these claustrophobic situations outside hospital,' he said helpfully. 'In a family, life can seem quite unbearable for some stupid reason that doesn't even give it the dignity of serious tragedy.'

Irene brushed aside his helpful suggestions, because she wanted to talk to him about the thing she had not been able to dislodge from her mind since Janice had talked to her about having children. She thought of him as a man of the world and, though it was embarrassing to broach such a subject with him, she felt sure he would not give her benign mealy-mouthed reassurance. 'All that gossip was so cruel because it bore no relation to reality,' she said. 'There is this sweet girl Janice in the hospital – you remember, we were talking about kitchen gadgets for her. Well, she took it into her head that you and I were planning to get married. She imagines we are both rich, so we wouldn't have any problems. What I mean is, even people who are ill like her can't imagine what it's like to be crippled at my age and to know that you'll never fall in love, never get married.'

'What makes you think you'll never fall in love?' he said slowly.

'Well, I suppose I could fall in love, but it would be just a crush and I'm too given to analysing my thoughts to fall very far.'

'You think you can avoid human folly just by analysing your thoughts?' he said.

'People can be so detached, watching themselves feeling things, so that they don't really feel them.' There was some annoyance in her voice. He didn't believe her and yet she was convinced that this would be her lot in life. 'Anyway, it's obvious no one's going to fall in love with me.'

'Why ever not?'

'In my condition,' she protested. She had expected an honest answer from him.

'You don't fall in love with a condition. Love is blind – have you never heard that? There are wheelchair marriages. I've seen them in the papers. They happen.'

'I couldn't do that,' she exclaimed. 'Someone who marries a cripple must have something wrong with him. He must need to be indispensable to someone. How could you take advantage of that? There's something morbid, unhealthy, in wanting to devote your whole life to a woman who's crippled. It's not a natural form of love – it's a travesty, a form of masochism. It's different for Janice – she was well when he married her. You ought to know what I mean,' she went on desperately, 'you said the same thing yourself. That sort of thing is more blessed to give than to receive.'

'My dear Irene,' he said. 'I can see I made a big mistake when I thought you were so wise, up there at your hospital window. You have a lot to learn about life and about love. There is so much you haven't yet experienced. Someone will fall in love with you against his will, against his better judgement. He'll think it quite out of the question to marry you, because you're crippled. He'll be a blessedly selfish, sensible person – a self-seeking rogue like myself. But he'll end up marrying you just because you're you and there's not another copy on the market in better condition. I promise you, you haven't seen all life yet, through your window.'

When he had told her she was wise, Irene had felt flattered, but doomed. Now that he'd changed his mind she felt relieved. 'Have I made a frightful fool of myself?' she asked with a sad little smile.

'Frightful,' he said. 'We've both been fools together, congratulating each other on being wise. Hadn't we better move out into the company of those ordinary optimistic fools with their faith in happy endings? Harriet has been preparing one of her sumptuous teas in the garden, with cream buns specially requested by me. Eunice doesn't let me have them every day any longer, and she's quite right of course – if I put on weight I shall overload Mr Harris's master work. I'll call them and they can come and fetch us.'